The Metamorphosis

and Related Readings

Glencoe McGraw-Hill

New York, New York   Columbus, Ohio   Woodland Hills, California   Peoria, Illinois

Acknowledgments

Grateful acknowledgment is given authors, publishers, photographers, museums, and agents for permission to reprint the following copyrighted material. Every effort has been made to determine copyright owners. In case of any omissions, the Publisher will be pleased to make suitable acknowledgments in future editions.

THE METAMORPHOSIS, by Franz Kafka. Translated by Joachim Neugroschel. Translation copyright © 1993, 1995 by Joachim Neugroschel. All rights reserved. Reprinted by arrangement with Scribner, An Imprint of Simon & Schuster, Inc.

Excerpt from "Letter to His Father" from LETTERS TO FRIENDS, FAMILY AND EDITORS, by Franz Kafka, translated by Richard and Clara Winston. Copyright © 1958 by Schocken Books, Inc. Reprinted by permission of Random House, Inc.

Excerpt from *Letters to Felice*, by Franz Kafka, translated by James Stern and Elizabeth Duckworth, edited by Erich Heller and Jugen Born. Copyright © 1967 by Schocken Books, Inc. Reprinted by permission of Random House, Inc.

"Duration of Childhood" and "Portrait of My Father as a Young Man" from *Ahead of All Parting: The Selected Poetry and Prose of Rainer Maria Rilke*. Edited and translated by Stephen Mitchell. Translation copyright © 1995 by Stephen Mitchell. Reprinted by permission of Random House, Inc.

"Gaston" by William Saroyan. Reprinted by permission of the Board of Trustees of Leland Stanford Junior University.

Cover Art: *Self Portrait*, 1973. Francis Bacon (1909–1992). English. 34.4 x 29.2 cm. Private Collection/Crane Kalman Gallery, London/Bridgeman Art Library.

Glencoe/McGraw-Hill

*A Division of The **McGraw·Hill** Companies*

Send all inquiries to:
Glencoe/McGraw-Hill
8787 Orion Place
Columbus, OH 43240

ISBN 0-02-817992-7
Printed in the United States of America
2 3 4 5 6 7 8 9 026 04 03 02 01 00

Contents

The Metamorphosis

Franz Kafka

Chapter One

Oᴺᴇ ᴍᴏʀɴɪɴɢ, ᴜᴘᴏɴ ᴀᴡᴀᴋᴇɴɪɴɢ from agitated dreams, Gregor Samsa found himself, in his bed, transformed into a monstrous vermin. He lay on his hard, armorlike back, and when lifting his head slightly, he could view his brown, vaulted belly partitioned by arching ridges, while on top of it, the blanket, about to slide off altogether, could barely hold. His many legs, wretchedly thin compared with his overall girth, danced helplessly before his eyes.

"What's happened to me?" he wondered. It was no dream. His room, a normal if somewhat tiny human room, lay quietly between the four familiar walls. Above the table, on which a line of fabric samples had been unpacked and spread out (Samsa was a traveling salesman), hung the picture that he had recently clipped from an illustrated magazine and inserted in a pretty gilt frame. The picture showed a lady sitting there upright, bedizened in a fur hat and fur boa, with her entire forearm vanishing inside a heavy fur muff that she held out toward the viewer.

Gregor's eyes then focused on the window, and the dismal weather—raindrops could be heard splattering on the metal ledge—made him feel quite melancholy.

"What if I slept a little more and forgot all about this nonsense," he thought. But his idea was impossible to carry out, for while he was accustomed to sleeping on his right side, his current state prevented him from getting into that position. No matter how forcefully he attempted to wrench himself over on his right side, he kept rocking back into his supine state. He must have tried it a hundred times, closing his eyes to avoid having to look at those wriggling legs, and he gave up only when he started feeling a mild, dull ache in his side such as he had never felt before.

"Oh, God," he thought, "what a strenuous profession I've picked! Day in, day out on the road. It's a lot more stressful than the work in the home office, and along with everything else I also have to put up with these agonies of traveling—worrying about making trains, having bad, irregular meals, meeting new people all the time, but never forming any lasting friendships that mellow into anything intimate. To hell with it all!"

Feeling a slight itch on his belly, he slowly squirmed along on his back toward the bedpost in order to raise his head more easily. Upon locating the itchy place, which was dotted with lots of tiny white specks that he could not fathom, he tried to to touch the area with one of his legs, but promptly withdrew it, for the contact sent icy shudders through his body.

He slipped back into his former position.

"Getting up so early all the time," he thought, "makes you totally stupid. A man has to have his sleep. Other traveling salesmen live like harem women. For instance, whenever I return to the hotel during the morning to write up my orders, those men are still having breakfast. Just let me try that with my boss; I'd be kicked out on the spot. And anyway, who knows, that might be very good for me. If I weren't holding back because of my parents, I would have given notice long ago, I would have marched straight up to the boss and told him off from the bottom of my heart. He would have toppled from his desk! Besides, it's so peculiar the way he seats himself on it and talks down to the employees from his great height, and we also have to get right up close because he's so hard of hearing. Well, I haven't abandoned all hope; once I've saved enough to pay off my parents' debt to him—that should take another five or six years—I'll go through with it no matter what. I'll make a big, clean break! But for now, I've got to get up, my train is leaving at five A.M."

And he glanced at the alarm clock ticking on the wardrobe. "God Almighty!" he thought. It was six-thirty, and the hands of the clock were calmly inching forward, it was even past the half hour, it was almost a quarter to. Could the alarm have failed to go off? From the bed, you could see that it was correctly set at four o'clock; it must have gone off. Yes, but was it possible to sleep peacefully through that furniture-quaking jangle? Well, fine, he had not slept peacefully, though probably all the more soundly. But what should he do now? The next train would be leaving at seven; and to catch it, he would have to rush like mad, and the samples weren't packed up yet, and he felt anything but fresh or sprightly. And even if he did catch the train, there would be no avoiding the boss's fulminations, for the errand boy must have waited at the five A.M. train and long since reported Gregor's failure to show up. The boy was the director's creature, spineless and mindless. Now what if Gregor reported sick? But that would be extremely embarrassing and suspect, for throughout his five years with the firm he had never been sick even once. The boss was bound to come over with the medical-plan doctor, upbraid the parents about their lazy son, and cut off all objections by referring to the doctor, for whom everybody in the world was in the best of health but work-shy. And besides, would the doctor be all that wrong in this case? Aside from his drowsiness, which was really superfluous after his long sleep, Gregor actually felt fine and was even ravenous.

As he speedily turned all these things over in his mind, but could not resolve to get out of bed—the alarm clock was just striking a quarter to seven—there was a cautious rap on the door near the top end of his bed.

"Gregor," a voice called—it was his mother—"it's a quarter to seven. Didn't you have a train to catch?"

The gentle voice! Gregor was shocked to hear his own response; it was unmistakably his earlier voice, but with a painful and insuppressible squeal blending in as if from below, virtually leaving words in their full clarity for just a moment, only to garble them in their resonance, so that you could not tell whether you had heard right. Gregor had meant to reply in detail and explain everything, but, under the circumstances, he limited himself to saying, "Yes, yes, thank you, Mother, I'm getting up."

Because of the wooden door, the change in Gregor's voice was probably not audible on the other side, for the mother was put at ease by his reassurance and she shuffled away. However, their brief exchange had made the rest of the family realize that Gregor, unexpectedly, was still at home, and the father was already at one side door, knocking weakly though with his fist: "Gregor, Gregor," he called, "what's wrong?" And after a short pause, he admonished him again, though in a deeper voice, "Gregor! Gregor!"

At the other side door, however, the sister plaintively murmured, "Gregor? Aren't you well? Do you need anything?"

Gregor replied to both sides, "I'm ready now," and by enunciating fastidiously with drawn-out pauses between words, he tried to eliminate anything abnormal from his voice. Indeed, the father returned to his breakfast; but the sister whispered, "Gregor, open up, I beg you." However, Gregor had absolutely no intention of opening up; instead, he praised the cautious habit he had developed during his travels of locking all doors at night, even in his home.

For now, he wanted to get up calmly and without being nagged, put on his clothes, above all have breakfast, and only then think about what to do next; for he realized he would come to no sensible conclusion by pondering in bed. He remembered that often, perhaps from lying awkwardly, he had felt a slight ache, which, upon his getting up, had turned out to be purely imaginary, and he looked forward to seeing today's fancies gradually fading away. He had no doubt whatsoever that the change in his voice was nothing but the harbinger of a severe cold, an occupational hazard of traveling salesmen.

Throwing off the blanket was quite simple; all he had to do was puff himself up a little, and it dropped away by itself. Doing anything else, however, was difficult, especially since he was so uncommonly broad. He would have needed arms and hands to prop himself up, and all he had was the numerous tiny legs that kept perpetually moving every which way but without his managing to control them. If he tried to bend a leg, it first straightened out; and if he finally succeeded in taking charge of it, the other legs meanwhile all kept carrying on, as if emancipated, in extreme and painful agitation. "Just don't dawdle in bed," Gregor told himself.

To start with, he wanted to get out of bed with the lower part of his body; but this portion, which, incidentally, he had not yet seen and could not properly visualize, proved too cumbersome to move—it went so slowly. And when eventually, having grown almost frantic, he gathered all his strength and recklessly thrust forward, he chose the wrong direction and slammed violently into the lower bedpost, whereupon the burning pain he then felt made him realize that the lower part of his body might be precisely the most sensitive, at least for now.

He therefore first tried to get his upper portion out of the bed, and to do so he cautiously turned his head toward the side of the mattress. This actually proved easy; and eventually, despite its breadth and weight, his body bulk slowly followed the twisting of his head. But when his head was finally looming over the edge of the bed, in the free air, he was scared of advancing any further in this manner; for if he ultimately let himself plunge down like this, only an outright miracle would prevent injury to his head. And no matter what, he must not lose consciousness now of all times; he would be better off remaining in bed.

But when, sighing after repeating this exertion, he still lay there as before, watching his tiny legs battle each other perhaps even more fiercely and finding no way to bring peace and order to this idiosyncratic condition, he again mused that he could not possibly stay there. The most logical recourse would be to make any sacrifice whatsoever if there was even the slightest hope of his freeing himself from the bed. Yet at the same time, he did not neglect to keep reminding himself that a calm, indeed the calmest reflection was far superior to desperate resolves. In such moments, he fixed his eyes as sharply as he could on the window; but unfortunately, little comfort or encouragement could be drawn from the sight of the morning fog, which shrouded even the other side of the narrow street. "Already seven o'clock," he said to himself when the alarm clock struck again, "already seven o'clock and still such a thick fog." And for a short while, he lay quietly, breathing faintly, as if perhaps expecting the silence to restore real and normal circumstances.

But then he told himself, "I absolutely must be out of bed completely before the clock strikes seven-fifteen. Besides, by then someone from work will come to inquire about me, since the office opens before seven." And he now began seesawing the full length of his body at an altogether even rhythm in order to rock it from the bed. If he could get himself to tumble from the bed in this way, then he would no doubt prevent injury to his head by lifting it sharply while falling. His back seemed hard; nothing was likely to happen to it during the landing on the carpet. His greatest misgiving was about the loud crash that was sure to ensue, probably causing anxiety if not terror behind all the doors. Still, this risk had to be run.

By the time Gregor was already sticking halfway out of the bed (this new method was more of a game than a struggle, all he had to do was keep seesawing and wrenching himself along), it occurred to him how easy everything would be if someone lent him a hand. It would take only two strong people (he thought of his father and the maid); they would only have to slip their arms under his vaulted back, slide him out of the bed, crouch down with their burden, and then just wait patiently and cautiously as he flipped over to the floor, where he hoped his tiny legs would have some purpose. Now quite aside from the fact that the doors were locked, should he really call for assistance? Despite his misery, he could not help smiling at the very idea.

By now he was already seesawing so intensely that he barely managed to keep his balance, and so he would have to make up his mind very soon, for it was already ten after seven—when the doorbell rang. "It's someone from the office," he told himself, almost petrified, while his tiny legs only danced all the more hastily. For an instant, there was total hush. "They're not answering," Gregor said to himself, prey to some absurd hope. But then of course, the maid, as usual, strode firmly to the door and opened it. Gregor only had to hear the visitor's first word of greeting and he knew who it was—the office manager himself. Why oh why was Gregor condemned to working for a company where the slightest tardiness aroused the murkiest suspicions? Was every last employee a scoundrel, wasn't there a single loyal and dedicated person among them, a man who, if he failed to devote even a few morning hours to the firm, would go crazy with remorse, becoming absolutely incapable of leaving his bed? Wouldn't it suffice to send an office boy to inquire—if indeed this snooping were at all necessary? Did the office manager himself have to come, did the entire innocent family have to be shown that this was the only person who had enough brains to be entrusted with investigating this suspicious affair? And more because of these agitating reflections than because of any concrete decision, Gregor swung himself out of bed with all his might. There was a loud thud, but not really a crash. His fall was slightly cushioned by the carpet; and also, his back was more pliable than he had thought. Hence the dull thud was not so blatant. However, by not holding his head carefully enough, he had banged it; now he twisted it, rubbing it on the carpet in annoyance and pain.

"Something fell in there," said the office manager in the left-hand room. Gregor tried to imagine whether something similar to what had happened to him today might not someday happen to the office manager. After all, the possibility had to be granted. However, as if in brusque response to this question, the office manager now took a few resolute steps in the next room, causing his patent-leather boots to creak.

From the right-hand room, the sister informed Gregor in a whisper, "Gregor, the office manager is here."

"I know," said Gregor to himself, not daring to speak loudly enough for the sister to hear.

"Gregor," the father now said from the left-hand room, "the office manager has come to inquire why you didn't catch the early train. We have no idea what to tell him. Besides, he would like to speak to you personally. So please open the door. I'm sure he will be kind enough to overlook the disorder in the room."

"Good morning, Mr. Samsa," the office manager was calling amiably.

"He's not well," the mother said to the office manager while the father kept talking through the door, "he's not well, believe me, sir. Why else would Gregor miss a train! I mean, the boy thinks of nothing but his job. I'm almost annoyed that he never goes out in the evening; goodness, he's been back in town for a whole week now, but he's stayed in every single night. He just sits here at the table, quietly reading the newspaper or poring over timetables. The only fun he has is when he does some fretsawing. For instance, he spent two or three evenings carving out a small picture frame; you'd be amazed how pretty it is. It's hanging inside, in his room; you'll see it in a moment when Gregor opens the door. By the way, sir, I'm delighted that you're here; we could never have gotten Gregor to unlock the door by ourselves—he's so stubborn; and he must be under the weather, even though he denied it this morning."

"I'll be right there," said Gregor slowly and deliberately, but not stirring so as not to miss one word of the conversation.

"I can think of no other explanation either, Mrs. Samsa," said the manager, "I do hope it is nothing serious. Though still and all, I must say that for business reasons we businessmen—unfortunately or fortunately, as you will—very often must simply overcome a minor indisposition."

"Well, can the manager come into your room now?" asked the impatient father, knocking on the door again.

"No," said Gregor. In the left-hand room there was an embarrassed silence, in the right-hand room the sister began sobbing.

Why didn't she join the others? She had probably only just gotten out of bed and not yet started dressing. And what was she crying about? Because Gregor wouldn't get up and let the manager in, because he was in danger of losing his job, and because the boss would then go back to dunning Gregor's parents with his old claims? For the time being, those were most likely pointless worries. Gregor was still here and had no intention whatsoever of running out on his family. True, at this moment he was simply lying on the carpet, and no one aware of his condition would have seriously expected him to let in the manager. Indeed, Gregor could hardly be dismissed on the spot for this petty discourtesy, for which he would easily hit on an appropriate excuse later on. He felt it would make far more sense if they left him alone for now instead of pestering him with tears and coaxing. However, the others were in a state of suspense, which justified their behavior.

"Mr. Samsa," the manager now called out, raising his voice, "what is wrong? You are barricading yourself in your room, answering only 'yes' or 'no,' causing your parents serious and unnecessary anxieties, and —I only mention this in passing—neglecting your professional duties in a truly outrageous manner. I am speaking on behalf of your parents and the director of the firm and I am quite earnestly requesting an immediate and cogent explanation. I am dumbfounded, dumbfounded. I believed you to be a quiet, reasonable person, and now you suddenly seem intent on flaunting bizarre moods. This morning the director hinted at a possible explanation for your tardiness—it pertained to the cash collections that you were recently entrusted with—but in fact I practically gave him my word of honor that this explanation could not be valid. Now, however, I am witnessing your incomprehensible stubbornness, which makes me lose any and all desire to speak up for you in any way whatsoever. And your job is by no means rock solid. My original intention was to tell you all this in private, but since you are forcing me to waste my time here needlessly, I see no reason why your parents should not find out as well. Frankly, your recent work has been highly unsatisfactory. We do appreciate that this is not the season for doing a lot of business; still, there is no season whatsoever, there can be no season for doing no business at all, Mr. Samsa."

"But, sir," Gregor exclaimed, beside himself, forgetting everything else in his agitation, "I'll open the door immediately, this very instant. A slight indisposition, a dizzy spell have prevented me from getting up. I am still lying in bed. But now I am quite fresh again. I am getting out of bed this very second. Please be patient for another moment or two! It is not going as well as I expected. But I do feel fine. How suddenly it can overcome a person! Just last night I was quite well, my parents know I was—or rather, last night I did have a slight foreboding. It must have been obvious to anyone else. Just why didn't I report it at the office!? But one always thinks one can get over an illness without staying home. Sir! Please spare my parents! There are no grounds for any of the things you are accusing me of—in fact, no one has ever so much as breathed a word to me. Perhaps you have not seen the latest orders that I sent in. Anyhow, I *will* be catching the eight A.M. train, these several hours of rest have revitalized me. Do not waste any more of your time, sir; I'll be in the office myself instantly—please be kind enough to inform them of this and to give my best to the director!"

And while hastily blurting out all these things, barely knowing what he was saying, Gregor, most likely because of his practice in bed, had managed to get closer to the wardrobe and was now trying to pull himself up against it. He truly wanted to open the door, truly show himself and speak to the office manager; he was eager to learn what the others, who were so keen on his presence now, would say upon seeing him. If they were shocked, then Gregor would bear no further responsibility and could hold his peace. But if they accepted everything calmly, then he likewise had to reason to get upset, and could, if he stepped on it, actually be in the station by eight. At first, he kept sliding down the smooth side of the wardrobe, but eventually he gave himself a final swing and stood there ignoring the burning pains in his abdomen, distressful as they were. Next he let himself keel over against the back of a nearby chair, his tiny legs clinging to the edges. In this way, he gained control of himself and he kept silent, for now he could listen to the office manager.

"Did you understand a single word of that?" the office manager asked the parents. "He's not trying to make fools of us, is he?!"

"For goodness' sake," the mother exclaimed, already weeping, "he may be seriously ill and we're torturing him. Grete! Grete!" she then shouted.

"Mother?" the sister called from the other side. They were communicating across Gregor's room. "You have to go to the doctor immediately. Gregor is sick. Hurry, get the doctor. Did you hear Gregor talking just now?"

"That was an animal's voice," said the manager, his tone noticeably soft compared with the mother's shouting.

"Anna! Anna!" the father called through the vestibule into the kitchen, clapping his hands, "Get a locksmith immediately!" And the two girls, their skirts rustling, were already dashing through the vestibule (how could the sister have dressed so quickly?) and tearing the apartment door open. No one heard it slamming; they must have left it open, as is common in homes that are struck by disaster.

Gregor, however, had grown much calmer. True, the others no longer understood what he said even though it sounded clear enough to him, clearer than before, perhaps because his ears had gotten used to it. But nevertheless, the others now believed there was something not quite right about him, and they were willing to help. His spirits were brightened by the aplomb and assurance with which their first few instructions had been carried out. He felt included once again in human society and, without really drawing a sharp distinction between the doctor and the locksmith, he expected magnificent and astonishing feats from both. Trying to make his voice as audible as he could for the crucial discussions about to take place, he coughed up a little, though taking pains to do so quite softly, since this noise too might sound different from human coughing, which he no longer felt capable of judging for himself. Meanwhile, the next room had become utterly hushed. Perhaps the parents and the office manager were sitting and whispering at the table, perhaps they were all leaning against the doors and eavesdropping.

Gregor slowly lumbered toward the door, shoving the chair along, let go of it upon arriving, tackled the door, held himself erect against it—the pads on his tiny feet were a bit sticky—and for a moment he rested from the strain. But then, using his mouth, he began twisting the key in the lock. Unfortunately he appeared to have no real teeth—now with what should he grasp the key?—but to make up for it his jaws were, of course, very powerful. They actually enabled him to get the key moving, whereby he ignored the likelihood of his harming himself in some way, for a brown liquid oozed from his mouth, flowing over the key and dripping to the floor.

"Listen," said the office manager in the next room, "he's turning the key." This was very encouraging for Gregor; but everyone should have cheered him on, including the father and the mother. "Attaboy, Gregor!" they should have shouted. "Don't let go, get that lock!" And imagining them all as suspensefully following his efforts, he obliviously bit into the key with all the strength he could muster. In tune with his progress in turning the key, he kept dancing around the lock, holding himself upright purely by his mouth and, as need be, either dangling from the key or pushing it down again with the full heft of his body. It was the sharper click of the lock finally snapping back that literally brought Gregor to. Sighing in relief, he told himself, "So I didn't need the locksmith after all," and he put his head on the handle in order to pull one wing of the double door all the way in.

Since he had to stay on the same side as the key, the door actually swung back quite far without his becoming visible. He had to twist slowly around the one wing, and very gingerly at that, to avoid plopping over on his back before entering the next room. He was still busy performing this tricky maneuver, with no time to heed anything else, when he heard the office manager blurt out a loud "Oh!"—it sounded like a whoosh of wind—and now he also saw him, the person nearest to the door, pressing his hand to his open mouth and slowly shrinking back as if he were being ousted by some unseeable but relentless force. The mother, who, despite the office manager's presence, stood there with her hair still undone and bristling, first gaped at the father, clasping her hands, then took two steps toward Gregor and collapsed, her petticoats flouncing out all around her and her face sinking quite undetectably into her breasts. The father clenched his fist, glaring at Gregor as if trying to shove him back into his room, then peered unsteadily around the parlor before covering his eyes with his hands and weeping so hard that his powerful chest began to quake.

Gregor did not step into the parlor after all; instead he leaned against his side of the firmly bolted second wing of the door, so that only half his body could be seen along with his head, which tilted sideways above it, peeping out at the others. Meanwhile the day had grown much lighter. Across the street, a portion of the endless, grayish black building (it was a hospital) stood out clearly with its regular windows harshly disrupting the façade. The rain was still falling, but only in large, visibly separate drops that were also literally hurled separately to the ground. The breakfast dishes still abundantly covered the table because breakfast was the most important meal of the day for Gregor's father; and he would draw it out for hours on end by reading various newspapers. The opposite wall sported a photograph of Gregor from his military days: it showed him as a lieutenant, hand on sword, with a carefree smile, demanding respect for his bearing and his uniform. The vestibule door was open, and since the apartment door was open too, one could see all the way out to the landing and the top of the descending stairs.

"Well," said Gregor, quite aware of being the only one who had kept calm, "I'll be dressed in a minute, pack up my samples, and catch my train. Would you all, would you all let me go on the road? Well, sir, you can see I am not stubborn and I enjoy working. Traveling is arduous, but I could not live without it. Why, where are you going, sir? To the office? Right? Will you report all this accurately? A man may be temporarily incapacitated, but that is precisely the proper time to remember his past achievements and to bear in mind that later on, once the obstacle is eliminated, he is sure to work all the harder and more intently. After all, I am so deeply obligated to the director, you know that very well. And then, I have to take care of my parents and my sister. I'm in a tight spot, but still I'll work my way out again. So please don't make things more difficult for me than they already are. Put in a good word for me at the office! People don't like a traveling salesman, I know. They think he makes barrels of money and has a wonderful life. They simply have no special reason to examine their prejudice. But you, sir, you have a better notion of what it's all about than the rest of the staff, why, than even—this is strictly between us—a better notion than even the director, who, as owner of the firm, is easily swayed against an employee. You also know very well that a traveling salesman, being away from the office most of the year, can so easily fall victim to gossip, coincidences, and unwarranted complaints, and he cannot possibly defend himself since he almost never finds out about them, except perhaps when he returns from a trip, exhausted, and personally suffers their awful consequences at home without fathoming their inscrutable causes. Sir, please do not leave without saying something to show that you agree with me at least to some small extent!"

But the office manager had already turned away at Gregor's very first words, and he only looked back at him over his twitching shoulder and with gaping lips. Indeed during Gregor's speech, the manager did not halt for even an instant. Rather, without losing sight of Gregor, he retreated toward the door, but only very gradually, as if there were some secret ban on leaving the room. He was already in the vestibule, and to judge by his abrupt movement when he finally pulled his leg out of the parlor, one might have thought he had just burned the sole of his foot. In the vestibule, however, he stretched out his right hand very far, toward the staircase, as if some unearthly redemption were awaiting him there.

Gregor realized he must on no account allow the office manager to leave in this frame of mind; if he did, Gregor's position at the office would be thoroughly compromised. The parents did not quite understand this. During these long years, they had become convinced that he was set up for life at this firm, and besides they were so preoccupied with their immediate problems as to have lost all sense of foresight. Gregor, however, did possess such foresight. The office manager had to be held back, calmed down, cajoled, and finally won over; Gregor's future and that of his family hinged on it! If only the sister had been here! She was intelligent; she had already started to cry when Gregor was still lying calmly on his back. And the office manager, that ladies' man, would certainly have let her take him in hand: she would have shut the apartment door, kept him in the vestibule, and talked him out of his terror. But the sister was not there, so Gregor had to act on his own. Forgetting that he was as yet unacquainted with his current powers of movement and also that once again his words had possibly, indeed probably, not been understood, he left the wing of the door and lumbered through the opening. He intended to head toward the office manager, who was ludicrously clutching the banister on the landing with both hands. But Gregor, fumbling for support, yelped as he flopped down upon his many tiny legs. The instant this happened, he felt a physical ease and comfort for the first time that morning. His tiny legs had solid ground underneath, and he was delighted to note that they were utterly obedient—they even strove to carry him off to wherever he wished; and he already believed that the final recovery from all sufferings was at hand. He lay on the floor, wobbling because of his checked movement, not that far from his mother, who seemed altogether self-absorbed. But at that same moment, she unexpectedly leaped up, stretched her arms far apart, splayed her fingers, and cried, "Help! For God's sake, help!" Next she lowered her head as if to see Gregor more clearly, but then, in self-contradiction, she senselessly backed away, forgetting the covered table behind her, hurriedly sat down upon it without thinking, and apparently failed to notice that next to her the large coffeepot had been knocked over and was discharging a torrent of coffee full force upon the carpet

"Mother, Mother," Gregor murmured, looking up at her. For an instant, the office manager had entirely slipped his mind; on the other hand, Gregor could not help snapping his jaws a few times at the sight of the flowing coffee. This prompted the mother to scream again, flee from the table, and collapse into the father's arms as he came dashing up to her. But Gregor had no time for his parents: the office manager was already on the stairs; with his chin on the banister, he took one final look back. Gregor broke into a run, doing his best to catch up with him. The office manager must have had an inkling of this, for he jumped down several steps at a time and disappeared. However, he did shout, "Ugh!" and his shout rang through the entire stairwell.

Unfortunately, the father, who so far had stayed relatively composed, seemed thoroughly bewildered by the office manager's flight. For, instead of rushing after him or at least not preventing Gregor from pursuing him, the father, with his right hand, grabbed the cane that the office manager, together with a hat and overcoat, had forgotten on a chair and, with his left hand, took a large newspaper from the table. Stamping his feet, he brandished the cane and the newspaper at Gregor in order to drive him back into his room. No pleading from Gregor helped, indeed no pleading was understood; no matter how humbly Gregor turned his head, the father merely stamped his feet all the more forcefully. Across the room, the mother had flung open a window despite the cool weather, and leaning way out, she buried her face in her hands. A strong draft arose between the street and the stairwell, the window curtains flew up, the newspapers rustled on the table, stray pages wafted across the floor. The father charged pitilessly, spewing hisses like a savage. Since Gregor as yet had no practice in moving backwards, it was really slow going. Had he only been permitted to wheel around, he would have been inside his room at once. But he was afraid it would take too long, trying the father's patience even more—and at any moment now the cane in the father's hand threatened to deal the lethal blow to Gregor's back or head. Ultimately, however, Gregor had no choice, for he realized with dismay that he did not even know how to stay the course when backing up. And so, while constantly darting fearful side glances at his father, he began rotating as swiftly as he could, though he was actually very slow. Perhaps the father sensed Gregor's good intention, for he did not interfere—instead, he occasionally even steered the pivoting motion from a distance with the tip of his cane. If only the father would stop that unbearable hissing! It made Gregor lose his head altogether. He had swung around almost fully when, constantly distracted by those hisses, he actually miscalculated and briefly shifted the wrong way. And then, as soon as he finally managed to get his head to the doorway, his body proved too broad to squeeze through all that readily. Naturally, in the father's present mood, it never even remotely crossed his mind to push back the other wing of the door and create a passage wide enough for Gregor. He was obsessed simply with forcing Gregor back into his room as fast as possible. Nor would he ever have stood for the intricate preparations that Gregor needed for hoisting himself on end and perhaps passing through the doorway in that posture. Instead, as if there were no hindrance, the father drove Gregor forward with a great uproar: behind Gregor the yelling no longer sounded like the voice of merely one father. Now it was do or die, and Gregor—come what might—jammed into the doorway. With one side of his body heaving up, he sprawled lopsided in the opening. His one flank was bruised raw, ugly splotches remained on the white door, and he was soon wedged in and unable to budge on his own. The tiny legs on his one side were dangling and trembling in midair and the tiny legs on his other side were painfully crushed against the floor. But now the father gave him a powerful shove from behind—a true deliverance. And Gregor, bleeding heavily, flew far into his room. The door was slammed shut with the cane, and then the apartment was still at last.

Chapter Two

IT WAS ALMOST DUSK by the time Gregor emerged from his comatose sleep. He would certainly have awoken not much later even without being disturbed, for he felt sufficiently well rested; yet it seemed to him as if he had been aroused by fleeting steps and a cautious shutting of the vestibule door. The glow from the electric streetlamps produced pallid spots on the ceiling and the higher parts of the furniture, but down by Gregor it was dark. Slowly, still clumsily groping with his feelers, which he was just learn-ing to appreciate, he lumbered toward the door to see what had been going on. His left side appeared to be one long, unpleasantly tightening scar, and he actually had to limp on his two rows of legs. One tiny leg, moreover, had been badly hurt during that morning's events (it was almost miraculous that only one had been hurt) and it dragged along lifelessly.

Only upon reaching the door did Gregor discover what had actually en-ticed him: it was the smell of something edible. For there stood a bowl full of fresh milk with tiny slices of white bread floating in it. He practically chor-tled for joy, being even hungrier now than in the morning, and he promptly dunked his head into the milk until it was nearly over his eyes. Soon, how-ever, he withdrew his head in disappointment. Not only did the bruises on his left side make it difficult for him to eat—he could eat only if his entire wheezing body joined in—but he did not care for the milk, even though it had always been his favorite beverage, which was no doubt why his sister had placed it in his room. As a matter of fact, he turned away from the bowl almost with loathing and crawled back to the middle of the room.

In the parlor, as Gregor could see through the door crack, the gaslight was lit. But while at this time of day his father would usually take up his newspaper, an afternoon daily, and read it in a raised voice to the mother and sometimes also to the sister, not a sound was to be heard. Well, perhaps this practice of reading aloud, which the sister had always told Gregor about and written him about, had recently been discarded altogether. Yet while the entire apartment was hushed, it was anything but deserted.

"My, what a quiet life the family used to lead," Gregor thought to himself, and as he peered into the darkness, he felt a certain pride that he had managed to provide his parents and his sister with such a life in such a beautiful apartment. What if now all calm, all prosperity, all content-ment should come to a horrifying end? Rather than lose himself in such ruminations, Gregor preferred to start moving, and so he crept up and down the room.

Once, during the long evening, one side door and then the other was opened a tiny crack and quickly shut again: somebody had apparently felt an urge to come in, but had then thought the better of it. Gregor halted right at the parlor door, determined to somehow bring in the hesitant visitor or at least find out who it was. But the door was not reopened, and Gregor waited in vain. That morning, when the doors had been locked, everybody had wanted to come in; but now that he had opened one door, and the rest had clearly been opened during the day, nobody came, and the keys were on the other side.

It was not until late at night that the light in the parlor was put out. Gregor could easily tell that the parents and the sister had stayed up this long, for, as he could clearly discern, all three of them were tiptoeing off. Since nobody would be visiting Gregor until morning, he had lots of time to reflect undisturbed and to figure out how to restructure his life. But the free, high-ceilinged room where he was forced to lie flat on the floor terrified him without his being able to pinpoint the cause; after all, it was his room and he had been living there for the last five years. Turning half involuntarily and not without a faint sense of embarrassment, he scurried under the settee, where, even though his back was a bit squashed and he could not lift his head, he instantly felt very cozy, regretting only that his body was too broad to squeeze in all the way.

There he remained for the rest of the night, either drowsing and repeatedly yanked awake by his hunger, or else fretting amid vague hopes, all of which, however, led to his concluding that for now he would have to lie low and, by being patient and utterly considerate, help the family endure the inconveniences that, as it happened, he was forced to cause them in his present state.

By early morning—it was still almost night—Gregor had a chance to test the strength of the resolutions he had just made, for the sister, almost fully dressed, opened the vestibule door and suspensefully peered in. She did not find him right away, but when she noticed him under the settee (goodness, he had to be somewhere, he couldn't just have flown away), she was so startled that unable to control herself she slammed the door from the outside. But, apparently regretting her behavior, she instantly reopened the door and tiptoed in as if visiting a very sick patient or even a stranger. Gregor, having pushed his head forward to the very edge of the settee, was watching her. Would she notice that he had barely touched the milk, though by no means for lack of hunger, and would she bring in some other kind of food more to his taste? If she did not do so on her own, he would rather starve to death than point it out to her, even while he felt a tremendous urge to scoot out from under the settee, throw himself at her feet, and beg her for some good food. But the sister, with some surprise, instantly noticed the full bowl, from which only a little milk had splattered all around. She promptly picked up the bowl, though not with her bare hands, but with a rag, and carried it away. Gregor was extremely curious as to what she would replace it with, and all sorts of conjectures ran through his mind. But he would never have hit on what the sister actually did in the goodness of her heart. Hoping to check his likes and dislikes, she brought him a whole array of food, all spread out on an old newspaper. There were old, half-rotten vegetables, some bones left over from supper and coated with a solidified white sauce, a few raisins and almonds, some cheese that Gregor had declared inedible two days ago, dry bread, bread and butter, and salted bread and butter. Furthermore, along with all those things, she brought some water in the bowl, which had probably been assigned to Gregor for good. And sensing that Gregor would not eat in front of her, she discreetly hurried away, even turning the key, just to show him that he could make himself as comfortable as he wished. Gregor's tiny legs whirred as he charged toward the food. His wounds, incidentally, must have healed up by now, he felt no handicap anymore, which was astonishing; for, as he recalled, after he had nicked his finger with a knife over a month ago, the injury had still been hurting the day before yesterday. "Am I less sensitive now?" he wondered, greedily sucking at the cheese, which had promptly exerted a more emphatic attraction on him than any of the other food. His eyes watered with contentment as he gulped down the cheese, the vegetables, and the sauce in rapid succession. By contrast, he did not relish the fresh foods, he could not even stand their smells, and he actually dragged the things he wanted to eat a short distance away. He was already done long since and was simply lazing in the same spot when the sister, to signal that he should withdraw, slowly turned the key. Startled, he jumped up though he was almost dozing, and scuttered back under the settee. However, it took a lot of self-control to remain there even during the few short moments that the sister spent in the room, for his body was slightly bloated from the ample food and he could scarcely breathe in that cramped space. Amid short fits of suffocation, he stared with somewhat bulging eyes while the unsuspecting sister, wielding a broom, swept up not only the leftovers but also the untouched food, as if this too were now unusable; she then hastily dumped everything into a pail, shutting its wooden lid and carrying everything out. No sooner had she turned her back than he skulked out from under the settee and began stretching and puffing up.

That was how Gregor received his food every day: once in the morning, when the parents and the maid were still asleep, and the second time after the family lunch, for the parents would then take a brief nap while the sister would send the maid out on some errand. While the parents certainly did not want Gregor to starve either, they may not have endured knowing more about his eating than from hearsay, or the sister may have wished to spare them some—perhaps only slight—grief, for they were really suffering enough as it was.

Gregor could not find out what excuses they had come up with to get the doctor and the locksmith out of the apartment; for since he was not understood, no one, including the sister, assumed that he could understand them. And so, whenever she was in his room, he had to content himself with occasionally hearing her sighs and her appeals to the saints. It was only later, when she had gotten a bit accustomed to everything (naturally there could be no question of her ever becoming fully accustomed), Gregor sometimes caught a remark that was meant to be friendly or might be interpreted as such. "He certainly enjoyed it today," she would say when Gregor had polished off a good portion of the food; while in the opposite event, which was gradually becoming more and more frequent, she would say almost sadly: "Now once again nothing's been touched."

But while Gregor could learn no news directly, he would eavesdrop, picking up a few things from the adjacent rooms, and the instant he heard voices, he would promptly scuttle over to the appropriate door, squeezing his entire body against it. During the early period in particular, no conversation took place that was not somehow about him, even if only in secret. For two whole days, every single meal was filled with discussions about what they ought to do; but even between meals, they kept harping on the same theme, for there were always at least two family members in the apartment, since plainly nobody wished to stay home alone and they could by no means all go out at the same time. Furthermore, on the very first day, the maid— it was not quite clear how much she knew about what had occurred—had implored the mother on bended knees to dismiss her immediately. Then, saying goodbye a quarter hour later, she had tearfully thanked them for the dismissal as if it were the most benevolent deed that they had ever done for her; and without being asked, she had sworn a dreadful oath that she would never breathe a single word to anyone.

So now the sister, together with the mother, also had to do the cooking; but this was not much of a bother, for they ate next to nothing. Over and over, Gregor heard them urging one another to eat, though in vain, receiving no other answer than, "Thanks, I've had enough," or something similar. They may not have drunk anything either. The sister would often ask the father if he would like some beer and she warmly offered to go and get it herself; when he failed to respond, she anticipated any misgivings on his part by saying she could also send the janitor's wife. But then the father would finally utter an emphatic "No," and the subject was no longer broached.

In the course of the very first day, the father laid out their overall financial circumstances and prospects to both the mother and the sister. From time to time, he rose from the table to fetch some document or notebook from his small strongbox, which he had salvaged after the collapse of his business five years earlier. They heard him opening the complicated lock and then shutting it again after removing whatever he had been looking for. The father's explanations were to some extent the first pleasant news that Gregor got to hear since his imprisonment. He had been under the impression that the father had failed to rescue anything from his business—at least, the father had told him nothing to the contrary, nor, admittedly, had Gregor ever asked him. Gregor's sole concern at that time had been to do whatever he could to make the family forget as quickly as possible the business catastrophe that had plunged them all into utter despair. And so he had thrown himself into his job with tremendous fervor, working his way up, almost overnight, from minor clerk to traveling salesman, who, naturally, had an altogether different earning potential and whose professional triumphs were instantly translated, by way of commissions, into cash, which could be placed on the table at home for the astonished and delighted family. Those had been lovely times, and they had never recurred, at least not with that same luster, even though Gregor was eventually earning so much money that he was able to cover and indeed did cover all the expenditures of the family. They had simply grown accustomed to this, both the family and Gregor; they accepted the money gratefully, he was glad to hand it over, but no great warmth came of it. Only the sister had remained close to Gregor; and since she, unlike Gregor, loved music and could play the violin poignantly, he was secretly planning to send her to the conservatory next year regardless of the great expense that it was bound to entail and that would certainly be made up for in some other way. During Gregor's brief stays in the city, the conservatory was often mentioned in his talks with the sister, but only as a lovely dream that could never possibly be realized; nor did the parents care to hear these innocent references. But Gregor's ideas on the subject were very definite and he intended to make the solemn announcement on Christmas Eve.

Such were the thoughts, quite futile in his present condition, that ran through his mind as he clung upright to the door, eavesdropping. Sometimes he was so thoroughly exhausted that he could no longer listen. His head would then inadvertently bump against the door, but he promptly pulled it erect again; for even that slight tap had been heard in the next room, causing everyone to stop talking. "What's he up to now!?" the father would say after a while, obviously turning toward the door, and only then did the interrupted conversation gradually resume.

Gregor now learned precisely enough (for the father would often repeat his explanations, partly because he himself had not dealt with these matters in a long time and partly because the mother did not always understand everything right off) that despite the disaster, some assets, albeit a very tiny sum, had survived from the old days, growing bit by bit because of the untouched interest. Furthermore, since the money that Gregor had brought home every month (keeping only a little for himself) had never been fully spent, it had accumulated into a small principal. Gregor, behind his door, nodded eagerly, delighted at this unexpected thrift and prudence. Actually, he could have applied this surplus toward settling the father's debt to the director, thereby bringing the day when he could have been rid of that job a lot closer; but now, the way the father had arranged things was better, no doubt.

Of course this sum was by no means large enough for the family to live off the interest; it might suffice to keep them going for one, at most two years, and that was all. It was simply money that really should not be drawn on and that ought to be put aside for emergencies, while the money to live on had to be earned. But the father, though still healthy, was an old man, who had not done a lick of work in five years and in any case could not be expected to take on very much. During those five years, his first vacation in an arduous and yet unsuccessful life, he had grown very fat, becoming rather clumsy. And should perhaps the old mother go to work—she, who suffered from asthma, who found it strenuous just walking through the apartment, and who spent every other day on the sofa, gasping for air by the open window? Or should the sister go to work—she, who was still a child at seventeen and should certainly keep enjoying her lifestyle, which consisted of dressing nicely, sleeping late, lending a hand with the housekeeping, going out to a few modest amusements, and above all, playing the violin? At first, whenever the conversation turned to this need to earn money, Gregor would always let go of the door and throw himself on the cool leather sofa nearby, for he felt quite hot with shame and grief.

Often he would lie there all through the long night, not getting a wink of sleep and merely scrabbling on the leather for hours on end. Or else, undaunted by the great effort, he would shove a chair over to the window, clamber up to the sill, and, propped on the chair, lean against the panes, obviously indulging in some vague memory of the freedom he had once found by gazing out the window. For actually, from day to day, even the things that were rather close were growing hazier and hazier; he could no longer even make out the hospital across the street, the all-too-frequent sight of which he used to curse. And if he had not known for sure that he lived on Charlotte Street, a quiet but entirely urban thoroughfare, he might have believed that he was staring at a wasteland in which gray sky and gray earth blurred together indistinguishably. Only twice had the observant sister needed to see the chair standing by the window; now, whenever she tidied up the room she would push the chair back to the window—indeed, from then on she would even leave the inside casement ajar.

If only Gregor could have spoken to her and thanked her for everything she had to do for him, he would have endured her kind actions more readily; but instead they caused him great suffering. Of course, she tried to surmount the overall embarrassment as much as possible, and naturally, as time wore by, she succeeded more and more. However, Gregor too eventually gained a sharper sense of things. Her very entrance was already terrible for him. No sooner had she stepped in than, without even taking time to close the door—careful as she usually was to protect everyone else from seeing Gregor's room—she charged straight over to the window and, as if almost suffocating, yanked it open with hasty hands, lingering there briefly no matter how chilly the weather and inhaling deeply. This din and dashing terrified Gregor twice a day. Throughout her visits he would cower under the settee, fully realizing that she would certainly have preferred to spare him this disturbance if only she had been able to keep the window shut while staying in the same room with him.

Once—something like a month had passed since Gregor's metamorphosis, and there was truly no special reason why the sister should still be alarmed by his appearance—she turned up a bit earlier than usual and caught Gregor staring out the window, motionless and terrifyingly erect. He would not have been surprised if she had refused to come in since his position prevented her from opening the window immediately. But not only did she not come in, she actually recoiled and closed the door; an outsider might have honestly thought that Gregor had meant to ambush her and bite her. Naturally he hid under the settee at once, but then had to wait until noon for his sister to return, and she seemed far more upset than usual. It thus dawned on him that his looks were still unbearable to her and were bound to remain unbearable, which meant that it must have taken a lot of self-control for her not to run away upon glimpsing even the tiny scrap of his body that protruded from under the settee. So one day, hoping to spare her even this sight—the job took him four hours—he got the sheet on his back and lugged it over to the settee, arranging it in such a way that it concealed him entirely, thereby preventing the sister from seeing him even when she stooped down. After all, if she considered the sheet unnecessary, she could have removed it, for it was plain that Gregor could not possibly enjoy cutting himself off so thoroughly. But she left the sheet just as it was, and once, he even believed he caught a grateful glance when he cautiously lifted it a smidgen with his head to see how his sister was taking this innovation.

During the first two weeks, the parents could not get themselves to come into his room, and he often heard them expressing their great appreciation of the sister's efforts, whereas earlier they had often been cross with her for being, they felt, a somewhat useless girl. But now both the father and the mother would frequently wait outside Gregor's door while the sister tidied up inside, and upon reemerging, she promptly had to render a detailed account of what the room looked like, what Gregor had eaten, how he had behaved this time, and whether he was perhaps showing some slight improvement. The mother, incidentally, wanted to visit Gregor relatively soon. At first, the father and the sister tried to reason with her, and Gregor paid very close attention to their arguments, approving of them wholeheartedly. Later, however, the mother had to be held back forcibly, and when she then cried out, "Let me go to Gregor, he's my unhappy son! Don't you understand I have to go to him?" Gregor felt it might be a good idea if she did come in after all—not every day, naturally, but perhaps once a week: she was much better at everything than the sister, who, for all her courage, was still a child and might ultimately have taken on such a demanding task purely out of teenage capriciousness.

Gregor's wish to see his mother came true shortly. During the day, if only out of consideration for his parents, he did not want to appear at the window. On the other hand, he could not creep very far around the few square meters of the floor, he found it hard to lie still even at night, and eating soon gave him no pleasure whatsoever. So, for amusement, he got into the habit of prowling crisscross over the walls and ceiling. He particularly liked hanging from the ceiling. It was quite different from lying on the floor: he could breathe more freely and a faint tingle quivered through his body. In his almost blissful woolgathering up there, Gregor might, to his own surprise, let go and crash down on the floor. But since he naturally now controlled his body far more effectively than before, he was never harmed by that great plunge. The sister instantly noticed the new entertainment that Gregor had found for himself—after all, when creeping, he occasionally left traces of his sticky substance behind. And so, taking it into her head to enable Gregor to crawl over the widest possible area, she decided to remove the obstructive furniture—especially the wardrobe and the desk. However, there was no way she could manage this alone. She did not dare ask her father for help, and the maid would most certainly not have pitched in; for while this girl, who was about sixteen, had been valiantly sticking it out since the cook's departure, she had asked for the special favor of keeping the kitchen door locked all the time and opening it only when specifically called. As a result, the sister had no choice but to approach the mother one day during the father's absence. And indeed, with cries of joyful excitement, the mother came over, although falling silent at the door to Gregor's room. First, naturally, the sister checked inside to make sure everything was in order; only then did she let the mother enter. Gregor had hurriedly pulled the sheet lower and in tighter folds, truly making it look as if it had been tossed casually over the settee. This time, Gregor also refrained from peeping out from under the sheet: he would go without seeing the mother for now and was simply glad that she had come despite everything.

"Come on, he's out of sight," said the sister, evidently leading the mother by the hand. Gregor now heard the two delicate women pushing the very heavy old wardrobe from its place and the sister constantly insisting on doing the major share of the work, ignoring the warnings from the mother, who was afraid she would overexert herself. It took a very long time. After probably just a quarter hour of drudging, the mother said it would be better if they left the wardrobe here. For one thing, it was too heavy—they would not be done before the father's arrival; and if the wardrobe stood in the middle of the room, it would block Gregor's movements in all directions. Secondly, it was not at all certain that they were doing Gregor a favor by removing the furniture. She said that the opposite seemed to be the case, the sight of the bare wall literally made her heart bleed. And why wouldn't Gregor respond in the same way since he was long accustomed to the furniture and would therefore feel desolate in the empty room? "And isn't that," the mother concluded very softly (in fact, she persistently almost whispered, as if, not knowing Gregor's precise whereabouts, she wanted to keep him from hearing the very sound of her voice, convinced as she was that he did not understand the words), "and if we remove the furniture, isn't that like showing him that we've given up all hope of his improvement and that we're callously leaving him to his own devices? I believe it would be best if we tried to keep the room just as it was, so that when Gregor comes back to us he will find that nothing's been changed and it will be much easier for him to forget what happened."

Upon hearing the mother's words, Gregor realized that in the course of these two months the lack of having anyone to converse with, plus the monotonous life in the midst of the family, must have befuddled his mind, for there was no other way to account for how he could have seriously longed to have his room emptied out. Did he really want the warm room, so cozily appointed with heirlooms, transformed into a lair, where he might, of course, be able to creep, unimpeded, in any direction, though forgetting his human past swiftly and totally? By now, he was already on the verge of forgetting, and had been brought up sharply only by the mother's voice after not hearing it for a long time. Nothing should be removed, everything had to remain: he could not do without the positive effects of the furniture on his state of mind. And if the furniture interfered with his senselessly crawling about, then it was a great asset and no loss.

Unfortunately, the sister was of a different mind; in the discussions concerning Gregor, she had gotten into the habit—not without some justification, to be sure—of acting the great expert in front of the parents. So now the mother's advice was again reason enough for the sister to demand that they remove not only the wardrobe and the desk, in line with her original plan, but all the furniture except for the indispensable settee. Her resoluteness was, naturally, prompted not just by childish defiance and the unexpected self-confidence she had recently gained at such great cost. After all, she had observed that while he needed a lot of space to creep around in, Gregor, so far as could be seen, made no use whatsoever of the furniture. Perhaps, however, the enthusiasm of girls her age also played its part—an exuberance that they try to indulge every chance they get. It now inveigled Grete into making Gregor's situation even more terrifying, so she could do even more for him than previously. For most likely no one but Grete would ever dare venture into a room where Gregor ruled the bare walls all alone.

And so she dug in her heels, refusing to give in to the mother, who, apparently quite anxious and uncertain of herself in this room, soon held her tongue and, to the best of her ability, helped the sister push out the wardrobe. Well, Gregor could, if necessary, do without the wardrobe, but the desk had to remain. And no sooner had the squeezing, groaning women shoved the wardrobe through the doorway than Gregor poked his head out from under the settee to judge how he could intervene as cautiously and considerately as possible. But alas, it was precisely the mother who was the first to return while Grete was still in the next room, holding her arms around the wardrobe and rocking it back and forth by herself without, of course, getting it to budge from the spot. The mother, however, was not used to the sight of Gregor—it might sicken her. And so Gregor, terrified, scuttered backwards to the other end of the settee, but was unable to prevent the front of the sheet from stirring slightly. That was enough to catch the mother's eye. She halted, stood still for an instant, then went back to Grete.

Gregor kept telling himself that nothing out of the ordinary was happening, it was just some furniture being moved. But these comings and goings of the women, their soft calls to one another, the scraping of the furniture along the floor was, as he soon had to admit, like a huge rumpus pouring in on all sides. And no matter how snugly he pulled in his head and legs and pressed his body against the floor, he inevitably had to own up that he would not endure the hubbub much longer. They were clearing out his room, stripping him of everything he loved. They had already dragged away the wardrobe, which contained the fretsaw and other tools, and they were now unprying the solidly embedded desk, where he had done his assignments for business college, high school, why, even elementary school—and he really had no time to delve into the good intentions of the two women, whom, incidentally, he had almost forgotten about, for they were so exhausted that they were already laboring in silence, and all that could be heard was the heavy plodding of their feet.

And so, while the women were in the next room, leaning against the desk to catch their breath, he broke out, changing direction four times, for he was truly at a loss about what to rescue first—when he saw the picture of the woman clad in nothing but furs hanging blatantly on the otherwise empty wall. He quickly scrambled up to it and squeezed against the glass, which held him fast, soothing his hot belly. At least, with Gregor now covering it up, this picture would certainly not be carried off by anyone. He turned his head toward the parlor door, hoping to observe the women upon their return.

After granting themselves little rest, they were already coming back; Grete had put her arm around her mother, almost carrying her. "Well, what should we take next?" said Grete, looking around. At this point, her eyes met those of Gregor on the wall. It was no doubt only because of the mother's presence that she maintained her composure. Bending her face toward the mother to keep her from peering about, she said, although trembling and without thinking: "Come on, why don't we go back to the parlor for a moment?" It was obvious to Gregor that she wanted to get the mother to safety and then chase him down from the wall. Well, just let her try! He clung to his picture, refusing to surrender it. He would rather jump into Grete's face.

But Grete's words had truly unnerved the mother, who stepped aside, glimpsed the huge brown splotch on the flowered wallpaper, and cried out in a harsh, shrieking voice before actually realizing that this was Gregor, "Oh God, oh God!" With outspread arms as if giving up everything, she collapsed across the settee and remained motionless.

"Hey, Gregor!" the sister shouted with a raised fist and a penetrating glare. These were her first direct words to him since his metamorphosis. She ran into the next room to get some sort of essence for reviving the mother from her faint. Gregor also wanted to help (there was time enough to salvage the picture later), but he was stuck fast to the glass and had to wrench himself loose. He then also scurried into the next room as if he could give the sister some kind of advice as in earlier times, but then had to stand idly behind her while she rummaged through an array of vials. Upon spinning around, she was startled by the sight of him. A vial fell on the floor and shattered. A sliver of glass injured Gregor's face, and some corrosive medicine oozed from the sliver. Grete, without further delay, grabbed as many vials as she could hold and dashed over to the mother, slamming the door with her foot. Gregor was thus cut off from the mother, who might have been dying because of him; he had to refrain from opening the door lest he frighten away the sister, who had to remain with the mother. There was nothing he could do but wait, and so, tortured by self-rebukes and worries, he began to creep about—he crept over everything, walls, furniture, and ceiling, and finally, in his despair, when the entire room began whirling around him, he plunged down to the middle of the large table.

A short while passed, with Gregor lying there worn out. The entire apartment was still, which was possibly a good sign. Then the doorbell rang. The maid was, naturally, locked up in her kitchen, and so Grete had to go and answer the door. The father had come.

"What's happened?" were his first words; Grete's face must have revealed everything. She replied in a muffled voice, obviously pressing her face into his chest: "Mother fainted, but she's feeling better now. Gregor broke out."

"I expected it," said the father, "I kept telling you both, but you women refuse to listen."

It was clear to Gregor that the father had misinterpreted Grete's all-too-brief statement and leaped to the conclusion that Gregor had perpetrated some kind of violence. That was why he now had to try and placate the father, for he had neither the time nor the chance to enlighten him. He therefore fled to the door of his room, squeezing against it, so that the father, upon entering from the vestibule, could instantly see that Gregor had every intention of promptly returning to his room and that there was no need to force him back. All they had to do was open the door and he would vanish on the spot.

But the father was in no mood to catch such niceties. "Ah!" he roared upon entering, and his tone sounded both furious and elated. Gregor drew his head back from the door and raised it toward the father. He had really not pictured him as he was standing there now; naturally, because of his new habit of creeping around, Gregor had lately failed to concern himself with anything else going on in the apartment and he should actually have been prepared for some changes. And yet, and yet, was this still his father? The same man who used to lie buried in bed, exhausted, whenever Gregor started out on a business trip; who, whenever Gregor came home in the evening, would greet him, wearing a robe, in the armchair; who, being quite incapable of standing up, would only raise his arms as a sign of joy; and who, bundled up in his old overcoat, laboriously shuffled along during rare family strolls on a few Sundays during the year and on the highest holidays, always cautiously planting his cane, trudging a bit more slowly between Gregor and the mother (they were walking slowly as it was); and who, whenever he was about to say anything, nearly always halted and gathered the others around him? But now the father stood quite steady, in a snug blue uniform with gold buttons, such as attendants in banks wear; his heavy double chin unfurled over the high stiff collar of the jacket. From under his bushy eyebrows, the black eyes gazed fresh and alert; the once disheveled hair was now glossy, combed down, and meticulously parted. Removing his cap with its gold monogram, probably that of a bank, and pitching it in an arc the full length of the room over to the settee, he lunged toward Gregor, his face grim, his hands in his trouser pockets, the tails of his long uniform jacket swinging back. He himself most likely did not know what he had in mind; nevertheless he lifted his feet unusually high, and Gregor marveled at the gigantic size of his boot soles. But he did not dwell on this; after all, from the very first day of his new life, he had known that the father viewed only the utmost severity as appropriate for dealing with him. And so now Gregor scooted away, stopping only when the father halted, and skittering forward again the instant the father moved. In this way, they circled the room several times with nothing decisive happening; in fact, because of its slow tempo, the whole business did not even resemble a chase. That was why Gregor kept to the floor for now, especially since he feared that the father might view an escape to the walls or the ceiling as particularly wicked. Nevertheless, Gregor had to admit that he could not endure even this scurrying much longer, because for every step the father took, Gregor had to carry out an endless string of movements. He was already panting noticeably, just as his lungs had never been altogether reliable even in his earlier days. He was just barely staggering along, trying to focus all his strength on running, scarcely keeping his eyes open, feeling so numb that he could think of no other possible recourse than running, and almost forgetting that he was free to use the walls, which, however, were blocked here by intricately carved furniture bristling with sharp points and notches—when all at once a lightly tossed something flew down right next to him, barely missing him, and rolled on ahead of him. It was an apple. Instantly a second one flew after the first. Gregor halted, petrified. Any more running would be useless, for the father was dead set on bombarding him. He had filled his pockets with fruit from the bowl on the sideboard and, not taking sharp aim for the moment, was hurling apple after apple. Those small red apples ricocheted around the floor as if galvanized, colliding with one another. A weakly thrown apple grazed Gregor's back, sliding off harmlessly. Another one, however, promptly following it, actually dug right into his back. Gregor wanted to keep dragging himself along as though this startling and incredible pain would vanish with a change of location, yet he felt nailed to the spot and so he stretched out with all his senses in utter derangement. It was only with his final glance that he saw the door to his room burst open. The mother, wearing only a chemise (for the sister had undressed her to let her breathe more freely while unconscious), hurried out in front of the screaming sister and dashed toward the father. Stumbling over her unfastened petti-coats as they glided to the floor one by one, she pressed against the father, flung her arms around his neck in total union with him—but now Gregor's eyesight failed entirely—and, with her hands clutching the back of the father's head, she begged him to spare Gregor's life.

Chapter
Three

Gregor's serious injury, from which he suffered for over a month (since no one had the nerve to remove the apple, it stayed lodged in his flesh as a visible memento), apparently reminded even the father that Gregor, despite his now dismal and disgusting shape, was a member of the family and could not be treated like an enemy. Instead, familial obligations dictated that they swallow their repulsion and endure, simply endure.

Now Gregor's injury may have cost him some mobility, no doubt for good, impelling him to take long, long minutes to shuffle across his room like an old war invalid (there was no question of his creeping up the walls). Still, this worsening of his condition was, to his mind, more than made up for by the fact that every evening the parlor door, which he would watch sharply for one or two hours in advance, was opened, so that he, lying in the darkness of his room and invisible from the parlor, was allowed to see the entire family at the illuminated table and, by general consent as it were, listen to their talks—rather, that is, than eavesdropping as before.

Of course, these were no longer the lively exchanges of earlier days, which Gregor had always somewhat wistfully mused about in the tiny hotel rooms whenever he had wearily collapsed into the damp bedding. Now, the evenings were usually very hushed. The father would doze off in his armchair shortly after supper; the mother and the sister would urge one another to keep still. The mother, hunched way over beneath the light, would be sewing fine lingerie for a fashion boutique; the sister, having found a job as salesgirl, was studying shorthand and French every evening in hopes of perhaps eventually obtaining a better position. Sometimes the father would wake up and, as if unaware that he had been sleeping, would say to the mother: "How long you've been sewing again today!" and doze off again while mother and sister smiled wearily at each other.

In a kind of obstinacy, the father refused to take off his attendant's uniform at home; and while his robe dangled uselessly on the clothes hook, he would slumber in his chair, fully dressed, as if always on duty and at his superior's beck and call even here. And so, despite all the painstaking efforts of mother and sister, the uniform, which had not been brand-new in the first place, grew less and less tidy, and Gregor would often spend entire evenings gazing at this soiled and spotted garment, which shone with its always polished gold buttons, while the old man slept a very uncomfortable and yet peaceful sleep.

The instant the clock struck ten, the mother, by speaking softly to the father, tried to awaken him and talk him into going to bed, for after all, this was no way to get proper sleep, which the father, who had to start work at six A.M., badly needed. But with the obstinacy that had gotten hold of him upon his becoming a bank attendant, he would always insist on remaining at the table a bit longer even though he invariably nodded out and, moreover, could then be coaxed only with the greatest difficulty to trade the chair for the bed. No matter how much the mother and the sister cajoled and gently admonished him, he would shake his head slowly for a quarter of an hour, keeping his eyes shut and refusing to stand up. The mother would tug at his sleeve, whispering honeyed words into his ear, and the sister would leave her homework to help the mother; but none of this had any effect on the father. He would merely sink deeper into his chair. It was only when the women lifted him under his armpits that he would open his eyes, glance to and fro between mother and sister, and say: "What a life. This is my rest in my old days." And supporting himself on the two women, he would ponderously struggle to his feet as if being the greatest burden on himself, let the two women steer him to the door, wave them off upon arriving and trudge on unaided, while the mother hastily discarded her sewing and the daughter her pen in order to run after him and continue being helpful.

Who in this overworked and exhausted family had time to look after Gregor any more than was absolutely necessary? The household was reduced further; the maid was now dismissed after all, and a gigantic bony charwoman with white hair fluttering around her head would come every morning and evening to do the heaviest chores. Everything else was taken care of by the mother along with her great amount of needlework. It even happened that various items of family jewelry, which mother and sister had once blissfully sported at celebrations and festivities, were now being sold off, as Gregor learned in the evenings from the general discussions of the prices they had obtained. Their greatest persistent complaint, though, was that since they could hit on no way of moving Gregor, they could not give up this apartment, which was much too large for their present circumstances. Gregor, however, realized it was not just their consideration for him that held them back, for they could have easily transported him in a suitable crate with a couple of air holes in it. The main obstacle to the family's relocation was their utter despair and their sense of being struck by a misfortune like no one else among their friends and relatives. Whatever the world demands of poor people, they carried out to an extreme: the father fetched breakfast for the minor bank tellers, the mother sacrificed herself to make underwear for strangers, the sister, ordered around by customers, ran back and forth behind the counter. But those were the limits of the family's strength. And the injury in Gregor's back started hurting again whenever mother and sister, having returned from getting the father to bed, ignored their work as they huddled together cheek to cheek, and the mother, pointing toward Gregor's room, now said: "Close that door, Grete," so that Gregor was back in the dark, while the women in the next room mingled their tears or peered dry-eyed at the table.

Gregor spent his nights and days almost entirely without sleep. Occasionally he decided that the next time the door opened, he would take over the family's affairs as in the past. Now, after a long absence, the director and the office manager reappeared in his thoughts, the clerks and the trainees, the dim-witted errand boy, two or three friends from other companies, a chambermaid in a provincial hotel, a dear, fleeting memory, a milliner's cashier whom he had courted earnestly but too slowly—they all reappeared, mingling with strangers or forgotten people. Yet rather than helping him and his family, they were all unapproachable, and he was glad when they dwindled away. At other moments, he was in no mood to worry about his family—he was filled with sheer rage at being poorly looked after; and although unable to picture anything that might tempt his appetite, he did try to devise ways of getting into the pantry and, while not hungry, taking what was ultimately his due. No longer paying any heed to what might be a special treat for Gregor, the sister, before hurrying off to work in the morning and after lunch, would use her foot to shove some random food into Gregor's room. Then, in the evening, indifferent as to whether the food had been merely tasted or—most often the case—left entirely untouched, she would sweep it out with a swing of the broom. She would now tidy up the room in the evening, and she could not have done it any faster. Grimy streaks lined the walls, knots of dust and filth littered the floor. In the beginning, when the sister arrived, Gregor would station himself in such particularly offensive corners as if to chide her. But he could have waited there for weeks on end without her making any improvement; she certainly saw the dirt as clearly as he did, but she had simply made up her mind to leave it there. Nevertheless, with a touchiness that aside from being quite novel for her had actually seized hold of the entire family, she made sure that this tidying-up remained her bailiwick. Once, the mother had subjected Gregor's room to a major cleansing, which had required several buckets of water (the great dampness, of course, made Gregor ill, and afterwards he sprawled on the settee, embittered and immobile). But the mother's punishment was not long in coming. For that evening, the instant the sister noticed the change in Gregor's room, she ran, deeply offended, into the parlor, and

even though the mother raised her hands beseechingly, the sister had a crying fit. The father was, naturally, startled out of his armchair, and both parents gaped, at first in helpless astonishment, until they too started in: the
father upbraided the mother, on his right, for not leaving the cleaning to
the sister and he yelled at the sister, on his left, warning her that she would
never again be allowed to clean Gregor's room. The mother tried to drag the
father, who was beside himself with rage, into the bedroom; the sister, quak-
ing with sobs, kept hammering the table with her little fists; and Gregor
hissed loudly in his fury because no one thought of closing his door to shield
him from this spectacle and commotion.

But even if the sister, exhausted from her work at the shop, was fed up
with looking after Gregor as before, by no means did the mother have to
step in to keep Gregor from being neglected. For now the charwoman was
here. This old widow, who, with the help of her strong bone structure, must
have managed to overcome the worst things in her long life, felt no actual
repugnance toward Gregor. While not really snooping, she had once happened to open the door to his room and, at the sight of Gregor, who, completely caught off guard, began scrambling every which way even though no
one was chasing him, she had halted in astonishment with her hands folded
on her abdomen. Since then, she had never failed to quickly open the door
a crack every morning and evening and peep in on him. Initially, she would
even summon him with phrases that she must have considered friendly, like
"C'mon over, you old dung beetle!" or "Just look at the old dung beetle!"
But Gregor refused to respond to such overtures; he stayed motionless in his
place as though the door had not been opened. If only they had ordered this
charwoman to clean his room daily instead of letting her gratuitously dis-
turb him whenever the mood struck her! Early one morning, when a violent
rain, perhaps a sign of the coming spring, was pelting against the window-
panes, the charwoman launched into her phrases again. Gregor felt so bit-
terly provoked that he charged toward her as if to attack, albeit slowly and
feebly. But the charwoman, undaunted, merely heaved up a chair by the
door and stood there with her mouth open wide, obviously intending to
close it only when the chair in her hand smashed down into Gregor's back.
"So that's as far as you're going?" she asked when he shifted away, and she
calmly returned the chair to the corner.

Gregor was now eating next to nothing. It was only when he happened
to pass the food left for him that he would playfully take a morsel into his
mouth, keep it in for hours and hours, and then usually spit it out again. At
first, he thought that his anguish about the condition of his room was what
kept him from eating, but he very soon came to terms with those very
changes. The family had gotten used to storing things here that could not
be put anywhere else, and now there were many such items here, for they

had rented out one room of the apartment to three boarders. These earnest gentlemen—all three had full beards, as Gregor once ascertained through the crack of the door—were sticklers for order, not only in their room, but also, since they were lodging here, throughout the apartment, especially the kitchen. They could not endure useless, much less dirty refuse. Moreover, they had largely brought in their own household goods. For this reason, many of the family's belongings had become superfluous; but while they had no prospects of selling them, they did not want to throw them out either. All these items wound up in Gregor's room—as did the ash bucket and the garbage can from the kitchen. If anything was unusable at the moment, the charwoman, who was always in a mad rush, would simply toss it into Gregor's room; luckily, he mostly saw only the object in question and the hand that held it. She may have intended to come for these things in her own good time or dump them all out in one fell swoop; but instead, they re-mained wherever they happened to land, unless Gregor twisted his way through the clutter, making it shift. At first, he had no choice, there being nowhere else for him to crawl; but later on it got to be more and more fun, even if, dead-tired and mournful after such treks, he would lie unstirring for hours on end.

Since the boarders sometimes also ate their supper at home in the com-mon parlor, the door between that room and Gregor's would remain shut on those evenings. But Gregor easily did without the open door—after all, there had been evenings when he had not even taken advantage of it; in-stead, unnoticed by the family, he had crouched in the darkest nook of his room. Once, however, the charwoman had left the parlor door ajar, and it remained ajar even when the boarders came in that evening and the light was turned on. Settling down at the head of the table, where the father, the mother, and Gregor had eaten in earlier times, they unfolded their napkins and took hold of their knives and forks. Instantly the mother appeared in the kitchen doorway with a platter of meat and, right behind her, the sister with a heaping platter of potatoes. The steaming food gave off thick fumes. The platters were set down in front of the boarders, who bent over them as if to test the food before eating it; and indeed the man sitting in the middle, and apparently looked up to as an authority by the two others, cut up a piece of meat on the platter, clearly in order to determine whether it was tender enough or should perhaps be sent back to the kitchen. He was satis-fied, and so mother and sister, who had been watching in suspense, began to smile with sighs of relief.

The family itself ate in the kitchen. Nevertheless, before heading there, the father would stop off in the parlor, bowing once, with his cap in his hand, and circle the table. The boarders would all rise and mumble some-thing into their beards. Then, by themselves again, they would eat in almost total silence. It struck Gregor as bizarre that amid all the various and sundry noises of eating, he kept making out the noise of their chewing as if he were being shown that one needed teeth for eating and that one could accomplish nothing with even the most wonderful toothless jaws. "I do have an appetite," Gregor told himself, "but not for these foods. How well these boarders eat, and I'm starving to death!"

That very evening (Gregor could not recall hearing it all this time), the sound of the violin came from the kitchen. The boarders had already finished their supper. The middle one had pulled out a newspaper, giving the other two one page each; and now they were leaning back, reading and smoking. When the violin began to play, the boarders pricked up their ears, got to their feet, and tiptoed over to the vestibule doorway, crowding into it and remaining there.

They must have been overheard from the kitchen, for the father called: "Do you gentlemen mind the violin? We can stop it immediately."

"Quite the contrary," said the middle gentleman, "would the young lady care to come and play in this room, which is far more convenient and comfortable?"

"Oh, thank you," called the father as if he were the violinist. The gentlemen came back into the parlor and waited. Soon the father arrived with the music stand, the mother with the sheet music, and the sister with the violin. The sister calmly prepared everything for the playing. The parents, having never rented out rooms before, which was why they were being so overly courteous to the boarders, did not dare sit in their own chairs. The father leaned against the door, slipping his right hand between two buttons of his buttoned-up uniform jacket; the mother, however, was offered a chair by one gentleman and, leaving it where he happened to place it, she sat off to the side, in a corner.

The sister began to play; the father and the mother, on either side, closely followed the motions of her hands. Gregor, drawn to the playing, had ventured a bit further out, so that his head was already sticking into the parlor. He was hardly aware of his recent lack of consideration toward the others, although earlier he had prided himself on being considerate. For now more than ever he had reason to hide, thoroughly coated as he was with the dust that shrouded everything in his room, flurrying about at the vaguest movement. Furthermore, threads, hairs, and scraps of leftover food were sticking to his back and his sides, for he had become much too apathetic to turn over and scour his back on the carpet as he used to do several times a day. And so, despite his present state, he had no qualms about advancing a bit across the spotless parlor floor.

Nor, to be sure, did anyone take any notice of him. The family was engrossed in the violin playing; the boarders, in contrast, their hands in their trouser pockets, had initially placed themselves much too close to the sister's music stand so they could all read the score, which was bound to fluster her. As a result, half muttering with lowered heads, they soon retreated to the window, where they remained, with the father eyeing them uneasily. It now truly seemed more than obvious that their hope of listening to a lovely or entertaining violin recital had been dashed, that they had had enough of the performance, and that it was only out of sheer courtesy that they were allowing themselves to be put upon in their leisure. It was especially the manner in which they all blew their cigar smoke aloft through their mouths and noses that hinted at how fidgety they were. And yet the sister was playing so beautifully. Her face was leaning to the side, her sad, probing eyes were following the lines of notes. Gregor crawled a bit farther out, keeping his head close to the floor, so that their eyes might possibly meet. Was he a beast to be so moved by music? He felt as if he were being shown the path to the unknown food he was yearning for. He was determined to creep all the way over to the sister, tug at her skirt to suggest that she take her violin and come into his room, for no one here would reward her playing as he intended to reward it. He wanted to keep her there and never let her out, at least not in his lifetime. For once, his terrifying shape would be useful to him; he would be at all the doors of his room simultaneously, hissing at the attackers. His sister, however, should remain with him not by force, but of her own free will. She should sit next to him on the settee, leaning down to him and listening to him confide that he had been intent on sending her to the conservatory, and that if the misfortune had not interfered, he would have announced his plan to everyone last Christmas (Christmas was already past, wasn't it?), absolutely refusing to take "no" for an answer. After his declaration, the sister would burst into tears of emotion, and Gregor would lift himself all the way up to her shoulder and kiss her throat, which she had been keeping free of any ribbon or collar since she had first started working.

"Mr. Samsa!" the middle gentleman called to the father and, not wasting another word, pointed his index finger at Gregor, who was slowly edging forward. The violin broke off, the middle gentleman first smiled at his friends, shaking his head, and then looked back at Gregor. The father, instead of driving Gregor out, evidently considered it imperative first to calm the boarders, even though they were not the least bit upset and appeared to find Gregor more entertaining than the violin playing. The father hurried over to them and, with outspread arms, tried to push them into their room while simultaneously blocking their view of Gregor with his body. They now in fact began to grow a bit irate, though there was no telling whether it was due to the father's behavior or to their gradual realization that they had unknowingly had a neighbor like Gregor in the next room. They demanded explanations from the father, raised their arms like him, plucked at their beards, and only very slowly backed away toward their room. Meanwhile the sister had managed to overcome her bewilderment, caused by the abrupt end to her playing, and after a time of holding the violin and the bow in her slackly dangling hands and gazing at the score as if still playing, she suddenly pulled herself together, left the instrument in the mother's lap (she was still in her chair, her lungs heaving violently), and rushed into the next room, toward which the father was more and more forcefully herding the boarders. One could see the blankets and pillows in the beds flying aloft, then being neatly arranged under the sister's practiced hands. Before the gentlemen ever reached the room, she had finished making up the beds and slipped out. The father seemed once again so thoroughly overcome by his obstinacy that he neglected to pay the tenants the respect nevertheless due them. He merely kept shoving until the middle gentleman, who was already in the doorway of the room, brought him to a halt by thunderously stamping his foot. "I hereby declare," said the middle gentleman, raising his hand and looking around for the mother and the sister as well, "that in consideration of the repulsive conditions" (here he abruptly spit on the floor) "prevailing in this apartment and in this family, I am giving immediate notice in regard to my room. Naturally, I will not pay a single penny for the days I have resided here; on the other hand, I will give serious thought to the eventuality of pursuing some sort of claims against you, for which—believe me— excellent grounds can easily be shown." He paused and peered straight ahead as if expecting something. And indeed, his two friends promptly chimed in, saying, "We are giving immediate notice too." Thereupon he grabbed the doorknob and slammed the door with a crash.

The father, groping and staggering along, collapsed into his chair; he looked as if he were stretching out for his usual evening nap, but his head, dangling as if unsupported, revealed that he was anything but asleep. All this while, Gregor had been lying right where the boarders had first spotted him. His frustration at the failure of his plan, and perhaps also the feebleness caused by his persistent hunger, made it impossible for him to move. Dreading with some certainty that at any moment now he would have to bear the blame for the overall disaster, he waited. He was not even startled when the violin, sliding away from the mother's trembling fingers, plunged from her lap with a reverberating thud.

"My dear parents," said the sister, pounding her hand on the table by way of introduction, "things cannot go on like this. You may not realize it, but I do. I will not pronounce my brother's name in front of this monstrosity, and so all I will say is: We must try to get rid of it. We have done everything humanly possible to look after it and put up with it; I do not believe there is anything we can be reproached for."

"She couldn't be more right," said the father to himself. The mother, still struggling to catch her breath and with an insane look in her eyes, began to cough into her muffling hand.

The sister hurried over to the mother and held her forehead. The father, apparently steered to more concrete thoughts by the sister's words, sat bolt upright now, toying with his attendant's cap, which lay on the table, among the borders' leftover supper dishes. Every so often he glanced at Gregor, who kept silent.

"We've got to get rid of it," the sister now said exclusively to the father, for the mother heard nothing through her coughing, "it will kill the both of you, I can see it coming. People who have to work as hard as we do can't also endure this nonstop torture at home. I can't stand it anymore either." And she began sobbing so violently that her tears flowed down to the mother's face, from which she wiped them with mechanical gestures.

"But, child," said the father with compassion and marked understanding, "what should we do?"

The sister merely shrugged her shoulders to convey the perplexity that, in contrast with her earlier self-assurance, had overcome her as she wept.

"If he understood us," said the father, half wondering. The sister, in the thick of her weeping, wildly flapped her hand to signal that this was inconceivable.

"If he understood us," the father repeated, closing his eyes in order to take in the sister's conviction that this was impossible, "then perhaps we might come to some sort of terms with him. But as things are now—"

"It has to go," exclaimed the sister, "that's the only way, Father. You simply have to try and get rid of the idea that it is Gregor. Our real misfortune is that we believed it for such a long time. Just how can that possibly be Gregor? If that were Gregor, he would have realized long ago that human beings can't possibly live with such an animal and he would have left of his own accord. We might have no brother then, but we could go on living and honor his memory. Instead, this animal harries us, it drives out the boarders, it obviously wants to take over the whole apartment and make us sleep in the gutter. Look, Father," she suddenly screamed, "he's starting again!" And in a panic that Gregor could not for the life of him fathom, the sister actually deserted the mother. Literally thrusting away from her chair as if she would rather sacrifice her mother than remain near Gregor, she dashed behind the father, who, made frantic only by the sister's behavior, stood up, half raising his hands to shield her.

Yet Gregor never even dreamed of scaring anyone, least of all his sister. He had merely started wheeling around in order to lumber back to his room, although because of his sickly condition his movements did look peculiar, for he had to execute the intricate turns by repeatedly raising his head and banging it against the floor. He paused and looked around. His good intention seemed to have been recognized; the panic had only been momentary. Now they all gazed at him in dismal silence. The mother, stretching out her legs and pressing them together, sprawled in her chair, her eyes almost shut in exhaustion; the father and the sister sat side by side, she with her arm around his neck.

"Now maybe I can turn around," Gregor thought, resuming his labor. He could not help panting from the strain and he also had to rest intermittently. At least, no one was bullying him, and he was left to his own devices. Upon completing the turn, he headed straight back. Amazed that his room was far away, he could not understand how, given his feebleness, he had come this great distance almost unwittingly. But, absorbed in creeping rapidly, he scarcely noticed that no interfering word or outcry came from his family. It was only upon reaching the door that he turned his head—not all the way for he felt his neck stiffening; nevertheless, he did see that nothing had changed behind him, except that the sister had gotten to her feet. His final look grazed the mother, who was fast asleep by now.

No sooner was he inside his room than the door was hastily slammed, bolted, and locked. Gregor was so terrified by the sudden racket behind him that his tiny legs buckled. It was the sister who had been in such a rush. She had been standing there, waiting, and had then nimbly jumped forward, before Gregor had even heard her coming. "Finally!" she yelled to the parents while turning the key in the lock.

"What now?" Gregor wondered, peering around in the dark. He soon discovered that he could no longer budge at all. He was not surprised, it even struck him as unnatural that he had ever succeeded in moving on these skinny little legs. Otherwise he felt relatively comfortable. His entire body was aching, but it seemed to him as if the pains were gradually fading and would ultimately vanish altogether. He could barely feel the rotting apple in his back or the inflamed area around it, which were thoroughly cloaked with soft dust. He recalled his family with tenderness and love. His conviction that he would have to disappear was, if possible, even firmer than his sister's. He lingered in this state of blank and peaceful musing until the tower clock struck three in the morning. He held on long enough to glimpse the start of the overall brightening outside the window. Then his head involuntarily sank to the floor, and his final breath came feebly from his nostrils.

When the charwoman showed up early that morning (in her haste and sheer energy, and no matter how often she had been asked not to do it, she slammed all the doors so hard that once she walked in no peaceful sleep was possible anywhere in the apartment), and peeked in on Gregor as usual, she at first found nothing odd about him. Having credited him with goodness knows what brain power, she thought he was deliberately lying there so motionless, pretending to sulk. Since she happened to be clutching the long broom, she tried to tickle him from the doorway. This had no effect, and so she grew annoyed and began poking Gregor. It was only upon shoving him from his place but meeting no resistance that she became alert. When the true state of affairs now dawned on the charwoman, her eyes bulged in amazement and she whistled to herself. But instead of dawdling there, she yanked the bedroom door open and hollered into the darkness: "Go and look, it's croaked; it's lying there, absolutely croaked!"

Mr. and Mrs. Samsa sat upright in their matrimonial bed, trying to cope with the shock caused by the charwoman. When they managed to grasp what she meant, the two of them, one on either side, hastily clambered out of bed. Mr. Samsa threw the blanket over his shoulders, while Mrs. Samsa emerged in her nightgown; that was how they entered Gregor's room. Meanwhile, the door to the parlor, where Grete had been sleeping since the arrival of the boarders, had likewise opened; she was fully dressed and her face was pale as if she had not slept.

"Dead?" said Mrs. Samsa, quizzically eyeing the charwoman even though she could have gone to check everything for herself, or could have surmised it without checking.

"You bet," said the charwoman and by way of proof she thrust out the broom and pushed Gregor's corpse somewhat further to the side. Mrs. Samsa made as if to hold back the broom, but then let it be.

"Well," said Mr. Samsa, "now we can thank the Lord." He crossed himself and the three women imitated his example. Grete, her eyes glued to the corpse, said: "Just look how skinny he was. Well, he stopped eating such a long time ago. The food came back out exactly as it went in." And indeed, Gregor's body was utterly flat and dry; they realized this only now when it was no longer raised on its tiny legs and nothing else diverted their eyes.

"Grete, come into our room for a bit," said Mrs. Samsa, smiling wistfully, and Grete, not without looking back at the corpse, followed her parents into the bedroom. The charwoman closed the door to Gregor's room and opened the window all the way. Though it was still early morning, there was a touch of warmth in the fresh air. It was already late March, after all.

The three boarders stepped out of their room and, astonished, cast about for their breakfast; they had been forgotten. "Where is breakfast?" the middle gentleman peevishly asked the charwoman. But putting her finger on her lips, she hastily and silently beckoned for the gentlemen to come into Gregor's room. And come they did, and with their hands in the pockets of their somewhat threadbare jackets, they stood around Gregor's corpse in the now sunlit room.

Next, the bedroom door opened, and Mr. Samsa, in his livery, appeared with his wife on one arm and his daughter on the other. Their eyes were all slightly tearstained; now and then, Grete pressed her face into the father's arm.

"Leave my home at once!" Mr. Samsa told the three gentlemen, pointing at the door without releasing the women.

"What do you mean?" asked the middle gentleman, somewhat dismayed and with a sugary smile. The two other gentlemen held their hands behind their backs, incessantly rubbing them together as if gleefully looking forward to a grand argument that they were bound to win.

"I mean exactly what I said," replied Mr. Samsa, and with his two companions he made a beeline toward the tenant. The latter at first stood his ground, eyeing the floor as if his thoughts were being rearranged to form a new pattern in his head.

"Well, then we'll go," he said, looking up at Mr. Samsa as if, in a sudden burst of humility, he were requesting sanction even for this decision. Mr. Samsa, with bulging eyes, merely vouchsafed him a few brief nods. Thereupon the gentleman strode right into the vestibule. His two friends, who had been listening for a short while with utterly calm hands, now quite literally hopped after him as if fearing that Mr. Samsa might precede them into the vestibule and might thrust himself between them and their leader. Once in the vestibule, all three boarders pulled their hats from the coat rack, their canes from the umbrella stand, bowed wordlessly, and left the apartment. Impelled by a suspicion that proved to be thoroughly groundless, Mr. Samsa and the two women stepped out on the landing. As they leaned on the banister, they watched the three gentlemen marching down the long stairway slowly but steadily, vanishing on every floor in the regular twist of the staircase, and popping up again several moments later. The lower the gentlemen got, the more the Samsa family lost interest in them, and as a butcher's boy, proudly balancing a basket on his head, came toward the gentlemen and then mounted well beyond them, Mr. Samsa and the women left the banister, and as if relieved, they all returned to their apartment.

They decided to spend this day resting and strolling; not only had they earned this break from work, they absolutely needed it. And so they sat down at the table to write three letters of explanation: Mr. Samsa to his superiors, Mrs. Samsa to her customer, and Grete to her employer. As they were writing, the charwoman came in to tell them she was leaving, for her morning's work was done. The three letter writers at first merely nodded without glancing up; it was only when she kept hovering that they looked up in annoyance. "Well?" asked Mr. Samsa. The charwoman stood beaming in the doorway as if she were about to announce some great windfall for the family, but would do so only if they dragged it out of her. On her hat, the small, almost erect ostrich plume, which had annoyed Mr. Samsa throughout her service here, swayed lightly in all directions. "What can we do for you?" asked Mrs. Samsa, whom the charwoman respected the most.

"Well," the charwoman replied with such friendly chuckling that she had to break off, "listen, you don't have to worry about getting rid of that stuff in the next room. It's all been taken care of."

Mrs. Samsa and Grete huddled over their letters as if to keep writing: Mr. Samsa, aware that the charwoman was on the verge of launching into a blow-by-blow description, resolutely stretched out his arm to ward her off. Not being allowed to tell her story, she suddenly remembered that she was in an awful hurry, and clearly offended, she called out: "So long, everybody." She then vehemently whirled around and charged out the apartment with a horrible slam of the door.

"She'll be dismissed tonight," said Mr. Samsa, receiving no answer from his wife or his daughter, for the charwoman had ruffled the peace and quiet that they had barely gained. Standing up, the two women went over to the window and remained there, clasped in each other's arms. Mr. Samsa looked back from his chair and silently watched them for a while. Then he exclaimed: "Come on, get over here. Forget about the past once and for all. And show me a little consideration." The women, promptly obeying him, hurried over, caressed him, and swiftly finished their letters.

Then all three of them left the apartment together, which they had not done in months, and took the trolley out to the countryside beyond the town. The streetcar, where they were the only passengers, was flooded with warm sunshine. Leaning back comfortably in their seats, they discussed their future prospects and concluded that, upon closer perusal, these were anything but bad; for while they had never actually asked one another for any details, their jobs were all exceedingly advantageous and also promising. Naturally, the greatest immediate improvement in their situation could easily be brought about by their moving; they hoped to rent a smaller and cheaper apartment, but with a better location and altogether more practical than their current place, which had been found by Gregor. As they were conversing, both Mr. and Mrs. Samsa, upon seeing the daughter becoming more and more vivacious, realized almost in unison that lately, despite all the sorrows that had left her cheeks pale, she had blossomed into a lovely and shapely girl. Lapsing into silence and communicating almost unconsciously with their eyes, they reflected that it was high time they found a decent husband for her. And it was like a confirmation of their new dreams and good intentions that at the end of their ride the daughter was the first to get up, stretching her young body.

Related Readings

Franz Kafka

from

Letter to His Father

Although The Metamorphosis *is a work of fiction, it is rooted in Franz Kafka's real-life experiences. This selection from a letter that Kafka wrote to his father in 1919 (but never delivered) gives insight into the strained relationship between Gregor Samsa and his father.*

DEAREST FATHER,

You asked me recently why I maintain that I am afraid of you. As usual, I was unable to think of any answer to your question, partly for the very reason that I am afraid of you, and partly because an explanation of the grounds for this fear would mean going into far more details than I could even approximately keep in mind while talking. And if I now try to give you an answer in writing, it will still be very incomplete, because even in writing, this fear and its consequences hamper me in relation to you and because the magnitude of the subject goes far beyond the scope of my memory and power of reasoning.

To you the matter always seemed very simple, at least in so far as you talked about it in front of me, and indiscriminately in front of many other people. It looked to you more or less as follows: you have worked hard all your life, have sacrificed everything for your children, above all for me, consequently I have lived high and handsome, have been completely at liberty to learn whatever I wanted, and have had no cause for material worries, which means worries of any kind at all. You have not expected any gratitude for this, knowing what "children's gratitude" is like, but have expected at least some sort of obligingness, some sign of sympathy. Instead I have always hidden from you, in my room, among my books, with crazy friends, or with extravagant ideas. I have never talked to you frankly; I have never come to you when you were in the synagogue, never visited you at Franzensbad, nor indeed ever shown any family feeling; I have never taken any interest in the business or your other concerns; I left the factory on your hands and walked off; I encouraged Ottla[1] in her obstinacy, and never lifted a finger for you (never even got you a theater ticket), while I do everything for my friends. If you sum up your judgment of me, the result you get is that, although you don't charge me with anything downright improper or wicked (with the exception perhaps of my latest marriage plan), you do charge me with coldness, estrangement, and ingratitude. And, what is more, you charge me with it in such a way as to make it seem my fault, as though I might have been able, with something like a touch on the steering wheel, to make everything quite different, while you aren't in the slightest to blame, unless it be for having been too good to me.

This, your usual way of representing it, I regard as accurate only in so far as I too believe you are entirely blameless in the matter of our estrangement. But I am equally entirely blameless. If I could get you to acknowledge this, then what would be possible is—not, I think, a new life, we are both much too old for that—but still, a kind of peace; no cessation, but still, a diminution of your unceasing reproaches.

Oddly enough you have some sort of notion of what I mean. For instance, a short time ago you said to me: "I have always been fond of you, even though outwardly I didn't act toward you as other fathers generally do, and this precisely because I can't pretend as other people can." Now, Father, on the whole I have never doubted your goodness toward me, but this remark I consider wrong. You can't pretend, that is true, but merely for that reason to maintain that other fathers pretend is either mere opinionatedness, and as such beyond discussion, or on the other hand—and this in my view is what it really is—a veiled expression of the fact that something is wrong in our relationship and that you have played your part in causing it to be so, but without its being your fault. If you really mean that, then we are in agreement.

I'm not going to say, of course, that I have become what I am only as a result of your influence. That would be very much exaggerated (and I am indeed inclined to this exaggeration). It is indeed quite possible that even if I had grown up entirely free from your influence I still could not have become a person after your own heart. I should probably have still become a weakly, timid, hesitant, restless person, neither Robert Kafka nor Karl Hermann, but yet quite different from what I really am, and we might have got on with each other excellently. I should have been happy to have you as a friend, as a boss, an uncle, a grandfather, even (though rather more hesitantly) as a father-in-law. Only as a father you have been too strong for me, particularly since my brothers died when they were small and my sisters only

---

1. **Ottla** Ottilie, Franz's sister and the youngest of the Kafka children

came along much later, so that I alone had to bear the brunt of it—and for that I was much too weak.

Compare the two of us: I, to put it in a very much abbreviated form, a Löwy[2] with a certain basis of Kafka, which, however, is not set in motion by the Kafka will to life, business, and conquest, but by a Lowyish spur that impels more secretly, more diffidently, and in another direction, and which often fails to work entirely. You, on the other hand, a true Kafka in strength, health, appetite, loudness of voice, eloquence, self-satisfaction, worldly dominance, endurance, presence of mind, knowledge of human nature, a certain way of doing things on a grand scale, of course also with all the defects and weaknesses that go with these advantages and into which your temperament and sometimes your hot temper drive you. You are perhaps not wholly a Kafka in your general outlook, in so far as I can compare you with Uncle Philipp, Ludwig, and Heinrich. That is odd, and here I don't see quite clear either. After all, they were all more cheerful, fresher, more informal, more easygoing, less severe than you. (In this, by the way, I have inherited a great deal from you and taken much too good care of my inheritance, without, admittedly, having the necessary counterweights in my own nature, as you have.) Yet you too, on the other hand, have in this respect gone through various phases. You were perhaps more cheerful before you were disappointed by your children, especially by me, and were depressed at home (when other people came in, you were quite different); perhaps you have become more cheerful again since then, now that your grandchildren and your son-in-law again give you something of that warmth which your children, except perhaps Valli,[3] could not give you. In any case, we were so different and in our difference so dangerous to each other that if anyone had tried to calculate in advance how I, the slowly developing child, and you, the full-grown man, would stand to each other, he could have assumed that you would simply trample me underfoot so that nothing was left of me. Well, that did not happen. Nothing alive can be calculated. But perhaps something worse happened. And in saying this I would all the time beg of you not to forget that I never, and not even for a single moment, believe any guilt to be on your side. The effect you had on me was the effect you could not help having. But you should stop considering it some particular malice on my part that I succumbed to that effect.

I was a timid child. For all that, I am sure I was also obstinate, as children are. I am sure that Mother spoilt me too, but I cannot believe I was particularly difficult to manage; I cannot believe that a kindly word, a quiet taking by the hand, a friendly look, could not have got me to do anything

---

2. **Löwy** maiden name of Franz's mother, Julie Löwy
3. **Valli** Valerie, Franz's sister and the second youngest of the Kafka children

that was wanted of me. Now you are, after all, at bottom a kindly and soft-hearted person (what follows will not be in contradiction to this, I am speaking only of the impression you made on the child), but not every child has the endurance and fearlessness to go on searching until it comes to the kindliness that lies beneath the surface. You can only treat a child in the way you yourself are constituted, with vigor, noise, and hot temper, and in this case this seemed to you, into the bargain, extremely suitable, because you wanted to bring me up to be a strong, brave boy.

Your educational methods in the very early years I can't, of course, directly describe today, but I can more or less imagine them by drawing retrospective conclusions from the later years and from your treatment of Felix. What must be considered as heightening the effect is that you were then younger and hence more energetic, wilder, more untrammeled, and still more reckless than you are today and that you were, besides, completely tied to the business, scarcely able to be with me even once a day, and therefore made all the more profound an impression on me, never really leveling out into the flatness of habit.

There is only one episode in the early years of which I have a direct memory. You may remember it, too. One night I kept on whimpering for water, not, I am certain, because I was thirsty, but probably partly to be annoying, partly to amuse myself. After several vigorous threats had failed to have any effect, you took me out of bed, carried me out onto the *pavlatche*,[4] and left me there alone for a while in my nightshirt, outside the shut door. I am not going to say that this was wrong—perhaps there was really no other way of getting peace and quiet that night—but I mention it as typical of your methods of bringing up a child and their effect on me. I dare say I was quite obedient afterwards at that period, but it did me inner harm. What was for me a matter of course, that senseless asking for water, and the extraordinary terror of being carried outside were two things that I, my nature being what is was, could never properly connect with each other. Even years afterwards I suffered from the tormenting fancy that the huge man, my father, the ultimate authority, would come almost for no reason at all and take me out of bed in the night and carry me out on the *pavlatche*, and that meant I was a mere nothing for him.

That was only a small beginning, but this sense of nothingness that often dominates me (a feeling that is in another respect, admittedly, also a noble and fruitful one) comes largely from your influence. What I would have needed was a little encouragement, a little friendliness, a little keeping open of my road, instead of which you blocked it for me, though of course with the good intention of making me go another road. But I was not fit for

---

4. *pavlatche* Czech word for a long outdoor balcony overlooking a courtyard

that. You encouraged me, for instance when I saluted and marched smartly, but I was no future soldier, or you encouraged me when I was able to eat heartily or even drink beer with my meals, or when I was able to repeat songs, singing what I had not understood, or prattle to you using your own favorite expressions, imitating you, but nothing of this had anything to do with my future. And it is characteristic that even today you really only encourage me in anything when you yourself are involved in it, when what is at stake is your own sense of self-importance, which I damage (for instance by my intended marriage) or which is damaged in me (for instance when Pepa is abusive to me). Then I receive encouragement, I am reminded of my worth, the matches I would be entitled to make are pointed out to me, and Pepa is condemned utterly. But apart from the fact that at my age I am now almost quite unsusceptible to encouragement, what help could it be to be anyway, if it only comes when it isn't primarily a matter of myself at all?

At that time, and at that time in every way, I would have needed encouragement. I was, after all, weighed down by your mere physical presence. I remember, for instance how we often undressed in the same bathing hut. There was I, skinny, weakly, slight; you strong, tall, broad. Even inside the hut I felt a miserable specimen, and what's more, not only in your eyes but in the eyes of the whole world, for you were for me the measure of all things. But then when we stepped out of the bathing hut before the people, you holding me by my hand, a little skeleton, unsteady, barefoot on the boards, frightened of the water, incapable of copying your swimming strokes, which you, with the best of intentions, but actually to my profound humiliation, always kept on showing me, then I was frantic with desperation and at such moments all my bad experiences in all spheres fitted magnificently together. I felt best when you sometimes undressed first and I was able to stay behind in the hut alone and put off the disgrace of showing myself in public until at last you came to see what I was doing and drove me out of the hut. I was grateful to you for not seeming to notice my anguish, and besides, I was proud of my father's body. By the way, this difference between us remains much the same to this very day.

In keeping, furthermore, was your intellectual domination. You had worked your way so far up by your own energies alone, and as a result you had unbounded confidence in your opinion. That was not yet so dazzling for me as a child as later for the boy growing up. From your armchair you ruled the world. Your opinion was correct, every other was mad, wild, *meshugge*,[5] not normal. Your self-confidence indeed was so great that you had no need to be consistent at all and yet never ceased to be in the right. It did sometimes happen that you had no opinions whatsoever about a matter and as a result

---

5. *meshugge* Yiddish for *crazy*

all opinions that were at all possible with respect to the matter were necessarily wrong, without exception. You were capable, for instance, of running down the Czechs, and then the Germans, and then the Jews, and what is more, not only selectively but in every respect, and finally nobody was left except yourself. For me you took on the enigmatic quality that all tyrants have whose rights are based on their person and not on reason. At least so it seemed to me.

Franz Kafka

from
Letters to
Felice

Shortly before writing The Metamorphosis, *Franz Kafka met Felice Bauer, a young woman from Berlin to whom he eventually became engaged but never married. Included here are selections from letters that Kafka wrote to Felice while he was working on* The Metamorphosis.

November 17, 1912

Dearest, * * * I was simply too miserable to get out of bed. It also seemed to me that last night my novel[1] got much worse, and I lay in the lowest depths. * * * I'll write you again today, even though I still have to run around a lot and shall write down a short story that occurred to me during my misery in bed and oppresses me with inmost intensity.

Night of November 17–18, 1912

Dearest, it is now 1:30 in the morning, the story I proclaimed is a long way from being finished, not a line of the novel has been written today, I am going to bed with little enthusiasm. If only I had the night free and without lifting pen from paper could write through it till morning! That would be a lovely night.

November 18, 1912

I was just sitting down to yesterday's story with an infinite longing to pour myself into it, obviously stimulated by my despair. Harassed by so much, uncertain of you, completely incapable of coping with the office, in view of the novel's being at a standstill for a day with a wild desire to continue the new, equally cautionary story, for several days and nights worrisomely close to complete insomnia, and with some less important but still

---

1. *The Boy Who Sank Out of Sight.*

upsetting and irritating things in my head—in a word, when I went for my evening walk today, which is already down to half an hour, * * * I firmly decided that my only salvation was to write to a man in Silesia whom I got to know fairly well this summer and who, for entire long afternoons, tried to convert me to Jesus.

November 23, 1912

It is very late at night. I have put aside my little story, on which I really haven't done anything at all for two evenings now and which in the stillness is beginning to develop into a bigger story. Give it to you to read? How shall I do that, even if it were already finished? It is written quite illegibly, and even if that weren't an obstacle—for up until now I certainly haven't spoiled you with beautiful handwriting—I still don't want to send you anything to read. I want to read it aloud to you. Yes, that would be fine, to read this story aloud to you and be forced to hold your hand, for the story is a little horrible. It is called *The Metamorphosis*, it would give you a real scare. * * * I am too depressed now, and perhaps I shouldn't have written to you at all. But today the hero of my little story also had a very bad time, and yet this is only the latest rung of his misfortune, which is now becoming permanent.

November 24, 1912

What sort of exceptionally repulsive story is this, which I am now once again putting aside in order to refresh myself with thoughts of you. It has already advanced a bit past the half-way mark, and on the whole I am not dissatisfied with it; but it is infinitely repulsive; and such things, you see, rise up from the same heart in which you dwell and which you put up with as your dwelling place. But don't be unhappy about this, for who knows, the more I write and the more I free myself, the purer and more worthy of you I may become, but no doubt there is still a lot more of me to be gotten rid of, and the nights can never be long enough for this business which, incidentally, is extremely voluptuous.

November 24, 1912

Now that I've mentioned the trip to Kratzau, I can't get this annoying thought out of my head. My little story would certainly have been finished tomorrow, but now I have to leave at 6 tomorrow evening, arrive at Reichenberg at 10, an go on to Kratzau at 7 the next morning to appear in court.

November 25, 1912

Well, today, dearest, I have to put aside my story, which I didn't work on today nearly as much as yesterday, and on account of the damned Kratzau trip shelve it for a day or two. I'm so unhappy about this, even if, as I hope, the story won't suffer too much, though I still need another 3–4 evenings to finish it. By not "suffering too much," I mean that the story is, unfortunately, already damaged by my method of working on it. This kind of story should be written with at most one interruption, in two ten-hour bouts: then it would have the natural thrust and charge it had in my head last Sunday. But I don't have twice ten hours at my disposal. So one has to try to do the best one can, since the best has been denied to one. What a pity that I can't read it to you—a great pity—for example, every Sunday morning. Not in the afternoon, I wouldn't have time then, that's when I have to write to you.

November 26, 1912

It was a horrible trip, dearest. * * * One should never travel: better be insubordinate at the office if there's work to be done at home that requires all one's strength. This eternal worry, which, incidentally, I still have now, that the trip will harm my little story, that I won't be able to write any more, etc.

November 27, 1912

I sit here all alone in the night, and, as today and yesterday, haven't written particularly well—the story lurches forward rather drearily and monotonously, and the requisite clarity illuminates it only for moments. * * * Now, however, I was firmly determined to use [the Christmas vacation] just for my novel and perhaps even to finish it. Today, when the novel has lain quiet for over a week—and the new story, though nearing its end, has been trying to convince me for the past two days that I have gotten stuck—I really should have to keep to that decision even more firmly.

December 1, 1912

After concluding the struggle with my little story—a third section, however, quite definitely * * * the last, has begun to take shape—I must absolutely say good night to you, dearest.

December 1, 1912

Just a few words, it's late, very late, and tomorrow there's a lot of work to be done; I've finally caught fire a bit with my little story, my heart wants to drive me with its beating further into it. However, I must try to get myself out of it as best I can, and since this will be hard work, and it will be hours before I get to sleep, I must hurry to bed. * * * Dearest, I wish I could still say something amusing, but nothing occurs to me naturally; furthermore, on the last page of my story open before me all 4 characters are crying or at any rate are in a most mournful mood.

December 3, 1912

I really should have kept on writing all night long. It would have been my duty, for I'm right at the end of my little story, and uniformity and the fire of consecutive hours would do this ending an unbelievable amount of good. Who knows, besides, whether I shall still be able to write tomorrow after the reading,[2] which I'm cursing now. Nevertheless—I'm stopping, I won't risk it. As a result of my writing, which I haven't been doing by any means for long with this sort of coherence and regularity, I have turned from being a by no means exemplary but in some ways still quite useful employee * * * into a horror for my boss. My desk in the office was certainly never orderly, but now it is piled high with a chaotic heap of papers and files. I have a rough idea of whatever lies on top, but I suspect nothing down below except terrors. Sometimes I think I can almost hear myself being ground to bits by my writing, on the one hand, and by the office, on the other. Then, again, there are times when I keep them both relatively well-balanced, especially when at home I've written badly, but I'm afraid I am gradually losing this ability (I don't mean of writing badly).

Night of December 4–5, 1912

Oh dearest, infinitely beloved, it is really too late now for my little story, just as I feared it would be; it will stare up at the sky unfinished until tomorrow night.

Presumably during the night of December 5–6, 1912

Cry, dearest, cry, the time for crying has come! The hero of my little story died a little while ago. If it is of any comfort to you, learn now that he died peaceably enough and reconciled with everything. The story itself is not yet completely finished: I'm no longer in the right mood for it now, and I am leaving the ending for tomorrow. It is also already very late, and I had enough to do to get over yesterday's disturbance.[3] It's a pity that in many passages of the story my states of exhaustion and other interruptions and extraneous worries are clearly inscribed; it could certainly have been done more purely: this can be seen precisely from the charming pages. That is

---

2. **the reading** public reading of "The Judgment" that Kafka was invited to give at an event honoring Prague writers.

3. **yesterday's disturbance** probably a reference to his public reading of "The Judgment."

exactly this persistently nagging feeling: I myself, I, with the creative powers that I feel in me, quite apart from their strength and endurance, could in more favorable circumstances of life have achieved a purer, more compelling, better organized work than the one which now exists. It is the one feeling that no amount of reason can dissuade me of, despite the fact, of course, that it is none other than reason that is right—which says that, just as there are no circumstances other than real ones, one cannot take any other ones into account, either. However that may be, I hope to finish the story tomorrow and the day after tomorrow throw myself back onto the novel.

December 6–7, 1912

Dearest, listen now: my little story is finished, but today's ending does not make me happy at all; it really could have been better, no doubt about that.

**Rainer Maria
Rilke**

Duration of Childhood

*Like Franz Kafka, Rainer Maria Rilke (1875–1926) was
born into a German-Jewish family living in Prague. Rilke
is generally considered to be one of the greatest poets of
modern times. These poems explore the complex
relationship between parent and child.*

for E.M.

Long afternoons of childhood . . . . , not yet really
life; still only growing-time
that drags at the knees—, time of defenseless waiting.
And between what we will perhaps become
5   and this edgeless existence—: deaths,
uncountable. Love, the possessive, surrounds
the child forever betrayed in secret
and promises him to the future; which is not his own.

Afternoons that he spent by himself, staring
10   from mirror to mirror; puzzling himself with the riddle
of his own name: Who? Who?—But the others
come home again, overwhelm him.
What the window or path
or the mouldy smell of a drawer
15   confided to him yesterday: they drown it out and
        destroy it.
Once more he belongs to them.
As tendrils sometimes fling themselves out from the
        thicker
bushes, his desire will fling itself out
from the tangle of family and hang there, swaying in
        the light.

20 But daily they blunt his glance upon their inhabited
    walls—that wide innocent glance which lets dogs in
    and holds the tall flowers,
    still almost face to face.

    Oh how far it is
25 from this watched-over creature to everything that
        will someday
    be his wonder or his destruction.
    His immature strength
    learns cunning among the traps.

    But the constellation
30 of his future love has long
    been moving among the stars. What terror
    will tear his heart out of the track of its fleeing
    to place it in perfect submission, under the calm
    influence of the heavens?

**Rainer Maria
Rilke**

Portrait of My Father as a Young Man

In the eyes: dream. The brow as if it could feel
something far off. Around the lips, a great
freshness—seductive, though there is no smile.
Under the rows of ornamental braid
5   on the slim Imperial officer's uniform:
the saber's basket-hilt. Both hands stay
folded upon it, going nowhere, calm
and now almost invisible, as if they
were the first to grasp the distance and dissolve.
10   And all the rest so curtained with itself,
so cloudy, that I cannot understand
this figure as it fades into the background—.

Oh quickly disappearing photograph
in my more slowly disappearing hand.

William Saroyan

Gaston

Like The Metamorphosis, *"Gaston" is a highly imaginative story in which an insect plays a leading role. William Saroyan (1908–1981) was a popular American author who wrote a number of short stories, novels, and plays.*

THEY WERE TO EAT PEACHES, as planned, after her nap, and now she sat across from the man who would have been a total stranger except that he was in fact her father. They had been together again (although she couldn't quite remember when they had been together before) for almost a hundred years now, or was it only since day before yesterday? Anyhow, they were together again, and he was kind of funny. First, he had the biggest mustache she had ever seen on anybody, although to her it was not a mustache at all; it was a lot of red and brown hair under his nose and around the ends of his mouth. Second, he wore a blue-and-white striped jersey instead of a shirt and tie, and no coat. His arms were covered with the same hair, only it was a little lighter and thinner. He wore blue slacks, but no shoes and socks. He was barefoot, and so was she, of course.

He was at home. She was with him in his home in Paris, if you could call it a home. He was very old, especially for a young man—thirty-six, he had told her; and she was six, just up from sleep on a very hot afternoon in August.

That morning, on a little walk in the neighborhood, she had seen peaches in a box outside a small store and she had stopped to look at them, so he had bought a kilo.

Now, the peaches were on a large plate on the card table at which they sat.

There were seven of them, but one of them was flawed. It *looked* as good as the others, almost the size of a tennis ball, nice red fading to light green, but where the stem had been there was now a break that went straight down into the heart of the seed.

He placed the biggest and best-looking peach on the small plate in front of the girl, and then took the flawed peach and began to remove the skin.

When he had half the skin off the peach he ate that side, neither of them talking, both of them just being there, and not being excited or anything—no plans, that is.

The man held the half-eaten peach in his fingers and looked down into the cavity, into the open seed. The girl looked, too.

While they were looking, two feelers poked out from the cavity. They were attached to a kind of brown knob-head, which followed the feelers, and then two large legs took a strong grip on the edge of the cavity and hoisted some of the rest of whatever it was out of the seed, and stopped there a moment, as if to look around.

The man studied the seed dweller, and so, of course, did the girl.

The creature paused only a fraction of a second and then continued to come out of the seed, to walk down the eaten side of the peach to wherever it was going.

The girl had never seen anything like it—a whole big thing made out of brown color, a knob-head, feelers, and a great many legs. It was very active, too. Almost businesslike, you might say. The man placed the peach back on the plate. The creature moved off the peach onto the surface of the white plate. There it came to a thoughtful stop.

"Who is it?" the girl said.

"Gaston."

"Where does he live?"

"Well, he *used* to live in this peach seed, but now that the peach has been harvested and sold, and I have eaten half of it, it looks as if he's out of house and home."

"Aren't you going to squash him?"

"No, of course not, why should I?"

"He's a bug. He's *ugh.*"

"Not at all. He's Gaston the grand boulevardier."[1]

"Everybody hollers when a bug comes out of an apple, but you don't holler or *anything.*"

"Of course not. How would *we* like it if somebody hollered every time we came out of our house?"

"Why *would* they?"

"Precisely. So why should we holler at Gaston?"

"He's not the same as us."

"Well, not exactly, but he's the same as a lot of other occupants of peach seeds. Now, the poor fellow hasn't got a home, and there he is with all that pure design and handsome form, and nowhere to go."

"Handsome?"

---

1. *boulevardier* a man-about-town

"Gaston is just about the handsomest of his kind I've ever seen."

"What's he saying?"

"Well, he's a little confused. Now, inside that house of his he had everything in order. Bed here, porch there, and so forth."

"Show me."

The man picked up the peach, leaving Gaston entirely alone on the white plate. He removed the peeling and ate the rest of the peach.

"Nobody else I know would do that," the girl said. "They'd throw it away."

"I can't imagine why. It's a perfectly good peach."

He opened the seed and placed the two sides not far from Gaston. The girl studied the open halves.

"Is *that* where he lives?"

"It's where he used to live. Gaston is out in the world and on his own now. You can see for yourself how comfortable he was in there. He had everything."

"Now what has he got?"

"Not very much, I'm afraid."

"What's he going to do?"

"What are *we* going to do?"

"Well, we're not going to squash him, that's one thing we're not going to do," the girl said.

"What *are* we going to do, then?"

"Put him back?"

"Oh, *that* house is finished."

"Well, he can't live in our house, can he?"

"Not happily."

"Can he live in our house *at all?*"

"Well, he could *try*, I suppose. Don't you want to eat a peach?"

"Only if it's a peach with somebody in the seed."

"Well, see if you can find a peach that has an opening at the top, because if you can, that'll be a peach in which you're likeliest to find somebody."

The girl examined each of the peaches on the big plate.

"They're all shut," she said.

"Well, eat one, then."

"No. I want the same kind that you ate, with somebody in the seed."

"Well, to tell you the truth, the peach I ate would be considered a bad peach, so of course stores don't like to sell them. I was sold that one by mistake, most likely. And so now Gaston is without a home, and we've got six perfect peaches to eat."

"I don't want a perfect peach. I want a peach with people."

"Well, I'll go out and see if I can find one."

"Where will I go?"

"You'll go with me, unless you'd rather stay. I'll only be five minutes."

"If the phone rings, what shall I say?"

"I don't think it'll ring, but if it does, say hello and see who it is."

"If it's my mother, what shall I say?"

"Tell her I've gone to get you a bad peach, and anything else you want to tell her."

"If she wants me to go back, what shall I say?"

"Say yes if you want to go back."

"Do you want me to?"

"Of course not, but the important thing is what you want, not what I want."

"Why is *that* the important thing?"

"Because I want you to be where you want to be."

"I want to be here."

"I'll be right back."

He put on socks and shoes, and a jacket, and went out. She watched Gaston trying to find out what to do next. Gaston wandered around the plate, but everything seemed wrong and he didn't know what to do or where to go.

The telephone rang and her mother said she was sending the chauffeur to pick her up because there was a little party for somebody's daughter who was also six, and then tomorrow they would fly back to New York.

"Let me speak to your father," she said.

"He's gone to get a peach."

"*One* peach?"

"One with people."

"You haven't been with your father two days and already you *sound* like him."

"There *are* peaches with people in them. I know. I saw one of them come out."

"A *bug?*"

"Not a bug. Gaston."

"*Who?*"

"Gaston the grand something."

"Somebody else gets a peach with a bug in it, and throws it away, but not him. He makes up a lot of foolishness about it."

"It's not foolishness."

"All right, all right, don't get angry at me about a horrible peach bug of some kind."

"Gaston is right here, just outside his broken house, and I'm not angry at you."

"You'll have a lot of fun at the party."

"OK."

"We'll have fun flying back to New York, too."

"OK."

"Are you glad you saw your father?"

"Of course I am."

"Is he funny?"

"Yes."

"Is he crazy?"

"Yes. I mean, no. He just doesn't holler when he sees a bug crawling out of a peach seed or anything. He just looks at it carefully. But it *is* just a bug, isn't it, *really?*"

"That's all it is."

"And we'll *have* to squash it?"

"That's right. I can't wait to see you, darling. These two days have been like two years to me. Good-bye."

The girl watched Gaston on the plate, and she actually didn't like him. He was all *ugh*, as he had been in the first place. He didn't have a home anymore and he was wandering around on the white plate and he was silly and wrong and ridiculous and useless and all sorts of other things. She cried a little, but only inside, because long ago she had decided she didn't like crying because if you ever started to cry it seemed as if there was so much to cry about you almost couldn't stop, and she didn't like that at all. The open halves of the peach seed were wrong, too. They were ugly or something. They weren't clean.

The man bought a kilo of peaches but found no flawed peaches among them, so he bought another kilo at another store, and this time his luck was better, and there were two that were flawed. He hurried back to his flat and let himself in.

His daughter was in her room, in her best dress.

"My mother phoned," she said, "and she's sending the chauffeur for me because there's another birthday party."

"Another?"

"I mean, there's *always* a lot of them in New York."

"Will the chauffeur bring you back?"

"No. We're flying back to New York tomorrow."

"Oh."

"I liked being in your house."

"I liked having you here."

"Why do you live here?"

"This is my home."

"It's nice, but it's a lot different from our home."

"Yes, I suppose it is."

"It's kind of like Gaston's house."

"Where *is* Gaston?"

"I squashed him."

"Really? Why?"

"Everybody squashes bugs and worms."

"Oh. Well. I found you a peach."

"I don't want a peach anymore."

"OK."

He got her dressed, and he was packing her stuff when the chauffeur arrived. He went down the three flights of stairs with his daughter and the chauffeur, and in the street he was about to hug the girl when he decided he had better not. They shook hands instead, as if they were strangers.

He watched the huge car drive off, and then he went around the corner where he took his coffee every morning, feeling a little, he thought, like Gaston on the white plate.

from

Notes from the Underground

Fyodor Dostoyevsky

The works of Russian author Fyodor Dostoyevsky (1821–1891) anticipate many of the themes explored in modern world literature. In Notes from the Underground, *one of his most important and influential works, Doystoyevsky delves into the mind of a man who "many times tried to become an insect."*

I AM A SICK MAN. . . . I am a spiteful man. I am an unattractive man. I believe my liver is diseased. However, I know nothing at all about my disease, and do not know for certain what ails me. I don't consult a doctor for it, and never have, though I have a respect for medicine and doctors. Besides, I am extremely superstitious, sufficiently so to respect medicine, anyway (I am well-educated enough not to be superstitious, but I am superstitious). No, I refuse to consult a doctor from spite. That you probably will not understand. Well, I understand, it though. Of course, I can't explain who it is precisely that I am mortifying in this case by my spite: I am perfectly well aware that I cannot "pay out" the doctors by not consulting them; I know better than anyone that by all this I am only injuring myself and no one else. But still, if I don't consult a doctor it is from spite. My liver is bad, well—let it get worse!

I have been going on like that for a long time—twenty years. Now I am forty. I used to be in the government service, but am no longer. I was a spiteful official. I was rude and took pleasure in being so. I did not take bribes, you see, so I was bound to find a recompense in that, at least. (A poor jest, but I will not scratch it out. I wrote it thinking it would sound very witty; but now that I have seen myself that I only wanted to show off in a despicable way, I will not scratch it out on purpose!)

When petitioners used to come for information to the table at which I

sat I used to grind my teeth at them, and felt intense enjoyment when I succeeded in making anybody unhappy. I almost did succeed. For the most part
they were all timid people—of course, they were petitioners. But of the up-
pish ones there was one officer in particular I could not endure. He simply
would not be humble, and clanked his sword in a disgusting way. I carried
on a feud with him for eighteen months over that sword. At last I got the
better of him. He left off clanking it. That happened in my youth, though.

But do you know, gentlemen, what was the chief point about my spite?
Why, the whole point, the real sting of it lay in the fact that continually,
even in the moment of the acutest spleen, I was inwardly conscious with
shame that I was not only not a spiteful but not even an embittered man,
that I was simply scaring sparrows at random and amusing myself by it. I
might foam at the mouth, but bring me a doll to play with, give me a cup of
tea with sugar in it, and maybe I should be appeased. I might even be genuinely touched, though probably I should grind my teeth at myself afterwards and lie awake at night with shame for months after. That was my way.

I was lying when I said just now that I was a spiteful official. I was lying
from spite. I was simply amusing myself with the petitioners and with the officer, and in reality I never could become spiteful. I was conscious every moment in myself of many, very many elements absolutely opposite to that. I
felt them positively swarming in me, these opposite elements. I knew that
they had been swarming in me all my life and craving some outlet from me,
but I would not let them, would not let them, purposely would not let them
come out. They tormented me till I was ashamed: they drove me to convul-
sions and—sickened me, at last, how they sickened me! Now, are not you
fancying, gentlemen, that I am expressing remorse for something now, that I
am asking your forgiveness for something? I am sure you are fancying that
. . . However, I assure you I do not care if you are. . . .

It was not only that I could not become spiteful, I did not know how to
become anything; neither spiteful nor kind, neither a rascal nor an honest
man, neither a hero nor an insect. Now, I am living out my life in my corner, taunting myself with the spiteful and useless consolation that an intelligent man cannot become anything seriously, and it is only the fool who
becomes anything. Yes, a man in the nineteenth century must and morally
ought to be pre-eminently a characterless creature; a man of character, an
active man is pre-eminently a limited creature. That is my conviction of
forty years. I am forty years old now, and you know forty years is a whole
lifetime; you know it is extreme old age. To live longer than forty years is
bad manners, is vulgar, immoral. Who does live beyond forty? Answer that,
sincerely and honestly. I will tell you who do: fools and worthless fellows.
I tell all old men that to their face, all these venerable old men, all these
silver-haired and reverend seniors! I tell the whole world that to its face! I

have a right to say so, for I shall go on living to sixty myself. To seventy! To eighty! . . . Stay, let me take breath . . .

You imagine no doubt, gentlemen, that I want to amuse you. You are mistaken in that, too. I am by no means such a mirthful person as you imagine, or as you may imagine; however, irritated by all this babble (and I feel that you are irritated) you think fit to ask me who I am—then my answer is, I am a collegiate assessor. I was in the service that I might have something to eat (and solely for that reason), and when last year a distant relation left me six thousand roubles in his will I immediately retired from the service and settled down in my corner. I used to live in this corner before, but now I have settled down in it. My room is a wretched, horrid one in the outskirts of the town. My servant is an old country-woman, ill-natured from stupidity, and, moreover, there is always a nasty smell about her. I am told that the Petersburg climate is bad for me, and that with my small means it is very expensive to live in Petersburg. I know all that better than all these sage and experienced counsellors and monitors. . . . But I am remaining in Petersburg; I am not going away from Petersburg! I am not going away because . . . ech! Why, it is absolutely no matter whether I am going away or not going away.

But what can a decent man speak of with most pleasure?
Answer: Of himself.
Well, so I will talk about myself.

I want to tell you, gentlemen, whether you care to hear it or not, why I could not even become an insect. I tell you solemnly, that I have many times tried to become an insect. But I was not equal even to that. I swear, gentlemen, that to be too conscious is an illness—a real thorough-going illness. For man's everyday needs, it would have been quite enough to have the ordinary human consciousness, that is, half or a quarter of the amount which falls to the lot of a cultivated man of our unhappy nineteenth century, especially one who has the fatal ill-luck to inhabit Petersburg, the most theoretical and intentional town on the whole terrestrial globe. (There are intentional and unintentional towns.) It would have been quite enough, for instance, to have the consciousness by which all so-called direct persons and men of action live. I bet you think I am writing all this from affectation, to be witty at the expense of men of action; and what is more, that from ill-bred affectation, I am clanking a sword like my officer. But, gentlemen, whoever can pride himself on his diseases and even swagger over them?

Though, after all, everyone does do that; people do pride themselves on their diseases, and I do, maybe, more than anyone. We will not dispute it; my contention was absurd. But yet I am firmly persuaded that a great deal of consciousness, every sort of consciousness, in fact, is a disease. I stick to that. Let us leave that, too, for a minute. Tell me this: why does it happen that at the very, yes, at the very moments when I am most capable of feeling every refinement of all that is "sublime and beautiful," as they used to say at one time, it would, as though of design, happen to me not only to feel but to do such ugly things, such that . . . Well, in short, actions that all, perhaps, commit; but which, as though purposely, occurred to me at the very time when I was most conscious that they ought not to be committed. The more conscious I was of goodness and of all that was "sublime and beautiful," the more deeply I sank in to my mire and the more ready I was to sink in it altogether. But the chief point was that all this was, as it were, not accidental in me, but as though it were bound to be so. It was as though it were my most normal condition, as not in the least disease or depravity, so that at last all desire in me to struggle against this depravity passed. It ended by my almost believing (perhaps actually believing) that this was perhaps my normal condition. But at first, in the beginning, what agonies I endured in that struggle! I did not believe it was the same with other people, and all my life I hid this fact about myself as a secret. I was ashamed (even now, perhaps, I am ashamed): I got to the point of feeling a sort of secret, abnormal, despicable enjoyment in returning home to my corner on some disgusting Petersburg night, acutely conscious that that day I had committed a loathsome action again, that what was done could never be undone, and secretly, inwardly gnawing at myself for it, tearing and consuming myself till at last the bitterness turned into a sort of shameful accursed sweetness, and at last—into positive real enjoyment! Yes, into enjoyment, into enjoyment! I insist upon that. I have spoken of this because I keep wanting to know for a fact whether other people feel such enjoyment? I will explain; the enjoyment was just from the too intense consciousness of one's own degradation; it was from feeling oneself that one had reached the last barrier, that it was horrible, but that it could not be otherwise; that there was no escape for you; that you never could become a different man; that even if time and faith were still left you to change into something different you would most likely not wish to change; or if you did wish to, even then you would do nothing; because perhaps in reality there was nothing for you to change into.

And the worst of it was, and the root of it all, that it was all in accord with the normal fundamental laws of over-acute consciousness, and with the inertia that was the direct result of those laws, and that consequently one was not only unable to change but could do absolutely nothing. Thus it would follow, as the result of acute consciousness, that one is not to blame in being a scoundrel; as though that were any consolation to the scoundrel once he has come to realise that he actually is a scoundrel. But enough. . . . Ech, I have talked a lot of nonsense, but what have I explained? How is enjoyment in this to be explained? But I will explain it. I will get to the bottom of it! That is why I have take up my pen. . . .

I, for instance, have a great deal of *amour propre*.[1] I am as suspicious and prone to take offence as a humpback or a dwarf. But upon my word I sometimes have had moments when if I had happened to be slapped in the face I should, perhaps, have been positively glad of it. I say, in earnest, that I should probably have been able to discover even in that a peculiar sort of enjoyment—the enjoyment, of course, of despair; but in despair there are the most intense enjoyments, especially when one is very acutely conscious of the hopelessness of one's position. And when one is slapped in the face— why then the consciousness of being rubbed into a pulp would positively overwhelm one. The worst of it is, look at it which way one will, it still turns out that I was always the most to blame for in everything. And what is most humiliating of all, to blame for no fault of my own but, so to say, through the laws of nature. In the first place, to blame because I am cleverer than any of the people surrounding me. (I have always considered myself cleverer than any of the people surrounding me, and sometimes, would you believe it, have been positively ashamed of it. At any rate, I have all my life, as it were, turned my eyes away and never could look people straight in the face.) To blame, finally, because even if I had had magnanimity, I should only have had more suffering from the sense of its uselessness. I should certainly have never been able to do anything from being magnanimous—neither to forgive, for my assailant would perhaps have slapped me from the laws of nature, and one cannot forgive the laws of nature; nor to forget, for even if it were owing to the laws of nature, it is insulting all the same. Finally, even if I had wanted to be anything but magnanimous, had desired on the contrary to revenge myself on my assailant, I could not have revenged myself on any one for anything because I should certainly never have made up my mind to do anything, even if I had been able to. Why should I not have made up my mind? About that in particular I want to say a few words.

With people who know how to revenge themselves and to stand up for themselves in general, how is it done? Why, when they are possessed, let us suppose, by the feeling of revenge, then for the time there is nothing else but that feeling left in their whole being. Such a gentleman simply dashes straight for his object like an infuriated bull with its horns down, and nothing but a wall will stop him. (By the way: facing the wall, such gentlemen— that is, the "direct" persons and men of action—are genuinely nonplussed. For them a wall is not an evasion, as for us people who think and consequently do nothing; it is not an excuse for turning aside, an excuse for

---

1. *amour propre* French for *self-esteem*

which we are always very glad, though we scarcely believe in it ourselves, as a rule. No, they are nonplussed in all sincerity. The wall has for them something tranquillising, morally soothing, final—maybe even something mysterious . . . but of the wall later.)

Well, such a direct person I regard as the real normal man, as his tender mother nature wished to see him when she graciously brought him into being on the earth. I envy such a man till I am green in the face. He is stupid. I am not disputing that, but perhaps the normal man should be stupid, how do you know? Perhaps it is very beautiful, in fact. And I am the more persuaded of that suspicion, if one can call it so, by the fact that if you take, for instance, the antithesis of the normal man, that is, the man of acute consciousness, who has come, of course, not out of the lap of nature but out of a retort (this is almost mysticism, gentlemen, but I suspect this, too), this retort-made man is sometimes so nonplussed in the presence of his antithesis that with all his exaggerated consciousness he genuinely thinks of himself as a mouse and not a man. It may be an acutely conscious mouse, yet it is a mouse, while the other is a man, and therefore, et cætera, et cætera. And the worst of it is, he himself, his very own self, looks on himself as a mouse; no one asks him to do so; and that is an important point. Now let us look at this mouse in action. Let us suppose, for instance, that it feels insulted, too (and it almost always does feel insulted) and wants to revenge itself, too. There may even be a greater accumulation of spite in it than in *l'homme de la nature et de la vérité*. The base and nasty desire to vent that spite on its assailant rankles perhaps even more nastily in it than in *l'homme de la nature et de la vérité*. For through his innate stupidity the latter looks upon his revenge as justice pure and simple; while in consequence of his acute consciousness the mouse does not believe in the justice of it. To come at last to the deed itself, to the very act of revenge. Apart from the one fundamental nastiness the luckless mouse succeeds in creating around it so many other nastinesses in the form of doubts and questions, adds to the one question so many unsettled questions that there inevitably works up around it a sort of fatal brew, a stinking mess, made up of its doubts, emotions, and of the contempt spat upon it by the direct men of action who stand solemnly about it as judges and arbitrators, laughing at it till their healthy sides ache. Of course the only thing left for it is to dismiss all that with a wave of its paw, and, with a smile of assumed contempt in which it does not even itself believe, creep ignominiously into its mouse-hole. There in its nasty, stinking, underground home our insulted, crushed and ridiculed mouse promptly becomes absorbed in cold, malignant and, above all, everlasting spite. For forty years together it will remember its injury down to the smallest, most ignominious details, and every time will add, of itself, details still more ignominious, spitefully teasing and tormenting itself with its own imagination. It will itself be ashamed of its imaginings, but yet it will recall it all, it will go over and over every detail, it will invent unheard of things against itself, pretending that those things might happen, and will forgive nothing. Maybe it will begin to revenge itself, too, but, as it were, piecemeal, in trivial ways, from behind the stove, incognito, without believing either in its own right to vengeance, or in the success of its revenge, knowing that from all its efforts at revenge it will suffer a hundred times more than he on whom it revenges itself, while he, I daresay, will not even scratch himself. On its deathbed it will recall it all over again, with interest accumulated over all the years and . . .

But it is just in that cold, abominable half despair, half belief, in that conscious burying oneself alive for grief in the underworld for forty years, in that acutely recognised and yet partly doubtful hopelessness of one's position, in that hell of unsatisfied desires turned inward, in that fever of oscillations, of resolutions determined for ever and repented of again a minute later—that the savour of that strange enjoyment of which I have spoken lies. It is so subtle, so difficult of analysis, that persons who are a little limited, or even simply persons of strong nerves, will not understand a single atom of it. "Possibly," you will add on your own account with a grin, "people will not understand it either who have never received a slap in the face," and in that way you will politely hint to me that I, too, perhaps, have had the experience of a slap in the face in my life, and so I speak as one who knows. I bet that you are thinking that. But set your minds at rest, gentlemen, I have not received a slap in the face, though it is absolutely a matter of indifference to me what you may think about it. Possibly, I even regret, myself, that I have given so few slaps in the face during my life. But enough . . . not another word on that subject of such extreme interest to you.

I will continue calmly concerning persons with strong nerves who do not understand a certain refinement of enjoyment. Though in certain circumstances these gentlemen bellow their loudest like bulls, though this, let us suppose, does them the greatest credit, yet, as I have said already, confronted with the impossible they subside at once. The impossible means the stone wall! What stone wall? Why, of course, the laws of nature, the deductions of natural science, mathematics. As soon as they prove to you, for instance, that you are descended from a monkey, then it is no use scowling, accept it for a fact. When they prove to you that in reality one drop of your own fat must be dearer to you than a hundred thousand of your fellow-creatures, and that this conclusion is the final solution of all so-called virtues and duties and all such prejudices and fancies, then you have just to accept, there is no help for it, for twice two is a law of mathematics. Just try refuting it.

"Upon my word, they will shout at you, it is no use protesting: it is a case of twice two makes four! Nature does not ask your permission, she has nothing to do with your wishes, and whether you like her laws or dislike them, you are bound to accept her as she is, and consequently all her conclusions. A wall, you see, is a wall . . . and so on, and so on."

Merciful Heavens! but what do I care for the laws of nature and arithmetic, when, for some reason I dislike those laws and the fact that twice two makes four? Of course I cannot break through the wall by battering my head against it if I really have not the strength to knock it down, but I am not going to be reconciled to it simply because it is a stone wall and I have not the strength.

As though such a stone wall really were a consolation, and really did contain some word of conciliation, simply because it is as true as twice two makes four. Oh, absurdity of absurdities! How much better it is to understand it all, to recognise it all, all the impossibilities and the stone wall; not to be reconciled to one of those impossibilities and stone walls if it disgusts you to be reconciled to it; by the way of the most inevitable, logical combinations to reach the most revolting conclusions on the everlasting theme, that even for the stone wall you are yourself somehow to blame, though again it is as clear as day you are not to blame in the least, and therefore grinding your teeth in silent impotence to sink into luxurious inertia, brooding on the fact that there is no one even for you to feel vindictive against, that you have not, and perhaps never will have, an object for your spite, that it is a sleight of hand, a bit of juggling, a cardsharper's trick, that it is simply a mess, no knowing what and no knowing who, but in spite of all these uncertainties and jugglings, still there is an ache in you, and the more you do not know, the worse the ache.

"Ha, ha, ha! You will be finding enjoyment in toothache next," you cry, with a laugh.

"Well, even in toothache there is enjoyment," I answer. I had toothache for a whole month and I know there is. In that case, of course, people are not spiteful in silence, but moan; but they are not candid moans, they are malignant moans, and the malignancy is the whole point. The enjoyment of the sufferer finds expression in those moans; if he did not feel enjoyment in them he would not moan. It is a good example, gentlemen, and I will develop it. Those moans express in the first place all the aimlessness of your pain, which is so humiliating to your consciousness; the whole legal system of nature on which you spit disdainfully, of course, but from which you suffer all the same while she does not. They express the consciousness that you have no enemy to punish, but that you have pain; the consciousness that in spite of all possible Wagenheims you are in complete slavery to your teeth; that if someone wishes it, your teeth will leave off aching, and if he does not, they will go on aching another three months; and that finally if you are still contumacious and still protest, all that is left you for your own gratification is to thrash yourself or beat your wall with your fist as hard as you can, and absolutely nothing more. Well, these mortal insults, these jeers on the part of someone unknown, end at last in an enjoyment which sometimes reaches the highest degree of voluptuousness. I ask you gentlemen, listen sometimes to the moans of an educated man of the nineteenth century suffering from toothache, on the second or third day of the attack, when he is beginning to moan, not as he moaned on the first day, that is, not simply because he has toothache, not just as any coarse peasant, but as a man affected by progress and European civilisation, a man who is "divorced from the soil and the national elements," as they express it now-a-days. His moans become nasty, disgustingly malignant, and go on for whole days and nights. And of course he knows himself that he is doing himself no sort of good with his moans; he knows better than anyone that he is only lacerating and harassing himself and others for nothing; he knows that even the audience before whom he is making his efforts, and his whole family, listen to him with loathing, do not put a ha'porth of faith in him, and inwardly understand that he might moan differently, more simply, without trills and flourishes, and that he is only amusing himself like that from ill-humour, from malignancy. Well, in all these recognitions and disgraces it is that there lies a voluptuous pleasure. As though he would say: "I am worrying you, I am lacerating your hearts, I am keeping everyone in the house awake. Well, stay awake then, you, too, feel every minute that I have toothache. I am not a hero to you now, as I tried to seem before, but simply a nasty person, an impostor. Well, so be it, then! I am very glad that you see through me. It is nasty for you to hear my despicable moans: well, let it be nasty; here I will let you have a nastier flourish in a minute. . . ." You do not understand even now, gentlemen? No, it seems our development and our consciousness must go further to understand all the intricacies of this pleasure. You laugh? Delighted. My jests, gentlemen, are of course in bad taste, jerky, involved, lacking self-confidence. But of course that is because I do not respect myself. Can a man of perception respect himself at all?

Come, can a man who attempts to find enjoyment in the very feeling of his own degradation possibly have a spark of respect for himself? I am not saying this now from any mawkish kind of remorse. And, indeed, I could never endure saying, "Forgive me, Papa, I won't do it again," not because I am incapable of saying that—on the contrary, perhaps just because I have been too capable of it, and in what a way, too. As though of design I used to get into trouble in cases when I was not to blame in any way. That was the nastiest part of it. At the same time I was genuinely touched and penitent, I used to shed tears and, of course, deceived myself, though I was not acting in the least and there was a sick feeling in my heart at the time. . . . For that one could not blame even the laws of nature, though the laws of nature have continually all my life offended me more than anything. It is loathsome to remember it all, but it was loathsome even then. Of course, a minute or so later I would realise wrathfully that it was all a lie, a revolting lie, an affected lie, that is, all this penitence, this emotion, these vows of reform. You will ask why did I worry myself with such antics: answer, because it was very dull to sit with one's hands folded, and so one began cutting capers. That is really it. Observe yourselves more carefully, gentlemen, then you will understand that it is so. I invented adventures for myself and made up a life, so as at least to live in some way. How many times it has happened to me—well, for instance, to take offence simply on purpose, for nothing; and one knows oneself, of course, that one is offended at nothing; that one is putting it on, but yet one brings oneself at last to the point of being really offended. All my life I have had an impulse to play such pranks, so that in the end I could not control it in myself. Another time, twice, in fact, I tried hard to be in love. I suffered, too, gentlemen, I assure you. In the depth of my heart there was no faith in my suffering, only a faint stir of mockery, but yet I did suffer, and in the real, orthodox way; I was jealous, beside myself . . . and it was all from *ennui*,[2] gentlemen, all from *ennui*; inertia overcame me. You know the direct, legitimate fruit of consciousness is inertia, that is, conscious sitting-with-the-hands-folded. I have referred to this already. I repeat, I repeat with emphasis: all "direct" persons and men of action are active just because they are stupid and limited. How men of action are active just because they are stupid and limited. How explain that? I will tell you: in consequence of their limitation they take immediate and secondary causes for primary ones, and in that way persuade themselves more quickly and easily than other people do that they have found an infallible foundation for their activity, and their minds are at ease and you know that is the chief thing. To begin to act, you know, you must first have your mind completely at ease and no trace of doubt left in. Why, how am I, for example to set my mind at rest? Where are the primary causes on which I am to build? Where are my foundations? Where am I to get them from? I exercise myself in reflection; and consequently with me every primary cause at once draws after itself another still more primary, and so on to infinity. That is just the essence of every sort of consciousness and reflection. It must be a case of the laws of nature again. What is the result of it in the end? Why, just the same. Remember I spoke just now of vengeance. (I am sure you did not take it in.) I said that a man revenges himself because he sees justice in it. Therefore he has found a

---

2. *ennui* a state of extreme weariness or boredom

primary cause, that is, justice. And so he is at rest on all sides, and consequently he carries out his revenge calmly and successfully, being persuaded that he is doing a just and honest thing. But I see no justice in it, I find no sort of virtue in it either, and consequently if I attempt to revenge myself, it is only out of spite. Spite, of course, might overcome everything, all my doubts, and so might serve quite successfully in place of a primary cause, precisely because it is not a cause. But what is to be done if I have not even spite (I began with that just now, you know). In consequence again of those accursed laws of consciousness, anger in me is subject to chemical disintegration. You look into it, the object flies off into air, your reasons evaporate, the criminal is not to be found, the wrong becomes not a wrong but a phantom, something like the toothache, for which no one is to blame, and consequently there is only the same outlet left again—that is, to beat the wall as hard as you can. So you give it up with a wave of the hand because you have not found a fundamental cause. And try letting yourself be carried away by your feelings, blindly, without reflection, without a primary cause, repelling consciousness at least for a time; hate or love, if only not to sit with your hands folded. The day after tomorrow, at the latest, you will begin despising yourself for having knowingly deceived yourself. Result: A soap-bubble and inertia. Oh, gentlemen, do you know, perhaps I consider myself an intelligent man, only because all my life I have been able neither to begin nor to finish anything. Granted I am a babbler, a harmless vexatious babbler, like all of us. But what is to be done if the direct and sole vocation of every intelligent man is babble, that is, the intentional pouring of water through a sieve?